Baltimore Chronicles

Volume 2

Baltimore Chronicles

Volume 2

Treasure Hernandez

www.urbanbooks.net

Urban Books, LLC
78 East Industry Court
Deer Park, NY 11729

Baltimore Chronicles Volume 2 Copyright © 2011 Treasure
Hernandez

ISBN 13: 978-1-60162-429-1
ISBN 10: 1-60162-429-8

First Printing January 2011
Printed in the United States of America

10 9 8 7 6 5 4 3 2 1

Distributed by Kensington Publishing Corp.
Submit Wholesale Orders to:
Kensington Publishing Corp.
C/O Penguin Group (USA) Inc.
Attention: Order Processing
405 Murray Hill Parkway
East Rutherford, NJ 07073-2316
Phone: 1-800-526-0275
Fax: 1-800-227-9604

Baltimore Chronicles

Volume 2

Treasure Hernandez

Prologue

Tiphani called Scar. "It's done, baby," she said. "I made all of the calls. We will live happily ever after." She smiled as she spoke into the receiver. "I love you too," she added, closing her eyes.

After hanging up the telephone, she shrugged into her coat on her way to mail her packages. She grabbed her keys and stepped out her door. As she took her first step, she was hit from the side. She didn't even have time to scream before she was dragged away.

"In breaking news, police report that Assistant District Attorney Tiphani Fuller has been reported missing. Police fear Mrs. Fuller may be in grave danger because of her husband's alleged criminal associations. ADA Fuller is the estranged wife of embattled Maryland State Trooper, narcotics detective Derek Fuller. Fuller, the former leader of the State Troopers' Drug Enforcement Section, was in-

dicted by a grand jury last week on charges of conspiracy and first-degree murder. He is a suspect in the brutal murder of a DES officer. The officer's mutilated body was found outside of the home Fuller shared with a fellow officer. Detective Fuller, who is currently being held without bond, is also suspected of cutting deals with the Dirty Money Crew, a notorious drug syndicate headed up by the infamous Stephon "Scar" Johnson. Police would not confirm whether they believe ADA Fuller's disappearance is directly related to her husband's alleged crimes, but said they are putting out all of their manpower and resources to find her. The FBI is also involved. ADA Fuller was last seen dropping her children off to school two weeks ago. The children's whereabouts are not being disclosed, for their safety. We will continue to follow the story as it develops," the reporter said, staring into the camera.

Derek sat on one of the small, hard, plastic chairs in the dayroom of the protective segregation unit inside the Baltimore County jail. The room was pin-drop quiet. Everyone was interested in the infamous narco that sat right in the same jail with them; inmates and COs alike were glued to the television. In protective segregation Derek was surrounded by other corrupt cops under arrest, and other inmates who needed special protection. The warden knew there was no way Derek would survive in general population with people he had put behind bars.

Derek felt the heat of eyes on him, but at that point,

he didn't care who was around him in the hellhole of a jail. The air around him was thick and threatened to suffocate him, even after he had finally exhaled. He was watching the television so intently, he didn't even realize he was involuntarily holding his breath.

He flexed his jaw at the news of Tiphani's disappearance and at the sight of his old home on the news, outside which every broadcast news station in Baltimore, Maryland was posted.

Derek was immediately drawn back to a time when his life was almost perfect. The two of them had everything, and within a second, *Boom!* Their lives had exploded into chaos. Now, here he sat in jail for crimes he didn't commit. His wife was missing, feared dead, and their kids would surely end up in foster care.

He shook his head. What had he done to himself? To them? Just seeing his former home on the screen made his stomach muscles clench. What would happen to his kids? Where could Tiphani have gone? "She wouldn't just leave the kids like that," he mumbled under his breath. "Something had to happen to her." All of a sudden, a rush of anxiety filled his gut, and he raced for his open cell so he could throw up.

Derek had a fucked up feeling about this whole disappearance, and about everything in general that had happened thus far. He felt betrayed in more ways than one. He couldn't believe that his administrative leave had so quickly turned into an all-out witch-hunt against him, and now he sat rotting in a fucking jail cell with a bunch of trumped-up evidence compiled against him. The crimes he was accused of were unheard of, but Derek had been pegged as the scapegoat for the department for some reason.

Derek finished emptying his guts into the toilet and swiped the back of his hand over his lips, his mind crowded with thoughts of Tiphani. The news story had clearly shaken him. He had hoped that Tiphani would've come home by now. Every day that passed made it worse for her and damn sure made it bad for him. He had already been questioned about Tiphani's disappearance and didn't like the underlying innuendo in the voice of the detective who had interviewed him. It was like they were trying to blame him for her disappearance too. He had become so frustrated at the detective asking him the same question seventy-five different ways, he jumped into the detective's face, but the cocky detective still didn't back down.

"Mr. Fuller, we understand that you and your wife were going through a bitter and nasty divorce and custody battle," the detective had said, a sly smirk on his wrinkled, olive-colored face.

"Yeah. And what of it?" Derek squinted his eyes.

"Well, sometimes when things like that are going on, one spouse, you know, may . . ." The detective's voice trailed off like he wanted Derek to fill in the blank with some crazy shit.

Even though Derek knew all of the interrogation tricks, he couldn't keep his cool. Blood immediately rushed to his head. "I didn't have anything to do with my wife's disappearance!" he screamed, his face turning almost burgundy as his heart hammered against his chest bone. He was used to being on the other side of the table, doing the interrogating, and discovered he didn't like being interrogated himself.

"Mr. Fuller, we are just trying to run down any leads that may help us find your wife," the detective said, his paper-thin lips moving in slow motion.

Every word seemed like flashbulbs of light to Derek, with nonstop images of Tiphani and Scar fucking exploding in front of him.

"I'm stuck in this fucking hellhole because somebody wanted me out of their way. My wife needs to be found now! My kids are all alone," Derek croaked out, the tears burning his eyes, and a sharp pain gripping him around the throat.

He couldn't erase the images of Scar ramming his wife in and out. Tiphani's face contorted with pleasure, pleasure that Derek was never able to give her. Derek's heart was breaking all over again. This was all too fucking much to handle.

"We are trying to find her, but I will tell you now. If she has in fact been kidnapped, and ends up dead, it only makes you look worse," the detective had said, as he rose to leave.

Derek shook the memories of that interrogation from his mind. That was almost two weeks ago, and still Tiphani had not been found. He'd heard on one of the many news stories that Tiphani's cell phone was found on the side of I-95. Not a good sign.

The night he was visited by the detective, just like today, he hadn't slept for even one hour. He hadn't been able to concentrate since. *If Tiphani turns up dead, I can forget my freedom. They will believe it was me, no matter what I do or say,* Derek thought as he paced up and down the pod. Although Tiphani had cheated on him, basically the catalyst for his downward spiral, he still worried about her whereabouts. He had a recurring thought since he'd learned about her disappearance—*Scar could be the only person responsible for her kidnapping. He is the only muthafucka that would dare.*

And just like everything else that had gone wrong in Derek's life as of late, Scar was behind it. Derek couldn't believe he was being labeled a cop killer for Archie's murder. Now Tiphani was gone, and he appeared to be the only one with an ax to grind, the divorce and custody battle making him the prime suspect, since no one knew about her affair with Scar.

Derek put his head in his hands and rocked back and forth. "God, if You exist, please let her be alive," he whispered.

Rodriguez let a smile spread across her petite face. *This must be it. It's really about to happen for me,* she thought to herself as she walked with a pep of arrogance in her step. She felt overly confident as she followed Chief Hill down to his office. Rodriguez was sure the private meeting requested by the chief would be the first step to promoting her to DES lead detective permanently, to officially taking over Derek's role.

The two walked in silence, both deep in thought. Once they arrived in the chief's office, the chief walked over to his desk and sat down. Rodriguez noticed that the chief's face was emotionless. To say that he had a poker face would be an understatement.

Suddenly, shit didn't seem like Rodriguez had thought. Watching the chief take his seat, a feeling of dread washed over her. Maybe she was wrong about the purpose of this meeting. The chief looked like he was about to bite her head off. Rodriguez couldn't figure it out, so she waited for the ball to drop.

"Nice artwork," she said, gesturing toward the chief's collection of black art paintings. She was trying to lighten the mood in the room.

The chief nodded, but inside he was laughing. *This bitch really thinks I'm stupid.* "Look, I didn't call you here for a social love call or no shit like that," Chief Hill said. "Have a seat. You'll need it."

Rodriguez sat down across from the chief. She placed her hands under her thighs to keep them from trembling. She knew now that she was definitely wrong about the purpose of this meeting.

"Look, I don't know what you got going on, or what you had against Derek Fuller, but I know what you did," Chief Hill said, staring Rodriguez down. He stared at Rodriguez so hard, his dark-brown, almost black eyes dug imaginary holes into Rodriguez's face.

Rodriguez started to say, "I don't know what—"

The chief put his hand up and cut her off mid-sentence. "You don't know what I'm talking about? Is that what you were going to say? That's the best you could do? The best lie you can come up with? C'mon, my six-year-old can do better than that!" Chief Hill spat, growing angry, feeling like Rodriguez thought he was stupid. More than anything, the chief hated to feel like somebody was trying to insult his intelligence.

"You fuckin' changed evidence in Fuller's case! Not only did you change it, you stole mitigating evidence that might help get him off! You also planted some shit," the chief said, letting Rodriguez know that she wasn't fooling him.

Rodriguez's face turned pale. It was like all of her color leaked from her face and pooled on the floor, buckets of sweat now dripping from her head. Rodriguez was frantic inside. She couldn't go out like this. *I'm taking shit to the grave*, she thought. She got defensive, the only way she figured she'd get around these accusations.

"You're fucking crazy!" she screamed, jumping up from the chair. "I would never do that shit! Fuller was my friend!"

"Sit the fuck down!" Chief Hill barked, the vein near his temple pulsing like crazy. "I'm not asking you if you did it. I know you did it!" He leaned back in his oversized leather chair and turned his computer monitor around so that the screen was facing Rodriguez.

Rodriguez swallowed hard, trying in vain to get rid of the huge lump that sat at the back of her throat. Finally able to breathe, she stood and stared at the monitor. She watched the computerized, grainy surveillance image of herself as she moved around the evidence cage. Her legs buckled, almost sending her five-foot seven-inch frame crashing to the floor.

"You look like you've seen a ghost. Sit down before you faint." The chief smirked. He had Rodriguez right where he wanted her—scared and willing to play the game.

Rodriguez flopped back down in the chair, exasperated and scared to death of what was about to come her way. "Chief, I swear . . ." Rodriguez started, her hands shaking so badly, she wanted to cut them off. Cold sweat now drenched her entire body, not just her head. Her bowels felt like they would release right there in her pants. This was the end of her career for sure, or so she thought.

"What made you do it? I mean, I thought Fuller was your friend . . . your supervisor and team member. I thought the DES was like a brotherhood? Didn't all you bastards go around professing this brotherhood shit?" Chief Hill shook his head left to right in a fake display of disgust.

Rodriguez hung her head at first. Then something hit her like a thunderbolt. "I—I was so mad about Archie's death. I mean, he didn't have to do him like that. His family couldn't even have an open casket. Then I started feeling like that mu'fucka Fuller had something to do with Bolden and Cassell's murders too. It was all too much to think about!!" Sweat dripped down her face, and she felt hot all over her body. She clenched her fists. At that moment, she wanted to see Derek in front of her. "I just wanted revenge. I didn't do it for any other reason, just revenge. I wanted him to suffer," Rodriguez fabricated on the spot.

"Bullshit! Nice acting job, Rodriguez." The chief smirked. "Scar Johnson is paying you too, ain't he?" Chief Hill stood up and leaned on his desk, toward Rodriguez. At that point, he was letting her know the gloves were off.

Rodriguez almost choked on her own tongue. *It's impossible for the chief to have figured that out,* she thought to herself. Rodriguez had only had one meeting with Scar, the initial meeting, and had always dealt with one of Scar's little workers when it came time to collect her money. There was no way Chief Hill would even associate her with Scar, unless he was on the fucking take himself.

"No. I don't know what you're talking about," Rodriguez lied, sticking to her take-it-to-the-grave philosophy.

"Don't bullshit me. I know all about it. See, I'm like God. Omniscient. I know everything that goes on in Baltimore," Chief Hill said, smiling evilly.

There was no need for her to continue fighting and denying her association. Her shoulders slumped, and she mentally gave up. It was time to level. "Please, Chief. This job is all I got. It's what I worked hard for all my life. I can't lose it. I can't afford to end up like Derek. I made a mistake . . . you gotta understand," Rodriguez pleaded, almost in tears.

"I hate to see a beautiful woman cry. Pull your skirt down and just fucking listen to what I have to say."

Rodriguez hung her head and listened. At this point, she didn't have a choice.

"I want twenty percent of whatever Scar is paying you, whenever he pays you. I want to know every time Scar contacts you. I will make sure my eyes and ears remain closed to what you're doing, but I expect my money. Don't ever think I can't find out how much you got, so make sure I get my twenty percent and you don't try to short me. We can all work together to bring Fuller down," Chief Hill said, leaning back in the chair in relax mode. "I never liked his ass anyway."

"Y-y-yes, sir, I can do that," Rodriguez stammered. She stood up and extended her hand toward the chief for a shake. "I can keep you posted, and the money is no problem. I can help you if you help me."

The chief accepted her hand, and they exchanged a brisk handshake, sealing their deal to help Scar put Derek away for life.

Chapter 1

The Best Laid Plans

Tiphani sat across from Scar and picked up her martini glass again. She was finally feeling a buzz. She still couldn't believe she was on a yacht, sailing off the coast of Florida toward the Caribbean. Scar sat across from her on a long black leather bench that was built into the yacht's upper deck wall. Tiphani stared at him with hazy eyes. She thought Scar looked hella sexy, rocking his Hermes boat shoes, a wife-beater that hugged his muscular chest, and a Gucci fedora sitting on top of his big head. She had conditioned herself to look past his ugly-ass scarred grill; his swagger was enough for her. It was more than her husband ever had.

Tiphani looked down at the feast set out in front of them. The table was full of all kinds of food prepared by Scar's own personal chef. There were lobster tails, huge freshly steamed shrimp surrounded by cocktail sauce, rich, leafy salads, tropical fruits, and the most expensive beluga caviar money could buy. Despite all of it, Tiphani hadn't touched a bite.

"Why you not eating?" Scar asked her, picking up one of the huge prawns, ready to throw it back.

"I'm not really that hungry," Tiphani said in a low tone, swirling her liquor around in her glass. She wasn't interested in the food, Scar, or anything on the yacht at this point. She was missing her kids and having second thoughts.

"Shit speak for yourself." Scar wasted no time digging into the food he'd paid a grip to have his chef cook up.

Tiphani took another sip of her drink. She ran her fingers through her long, jet-black hair, like she usually did when deep in thought. The sun was beginning to set, and her mood was continuing to go down right along with it. The sea breeze kissed her beautiful face and whipped around her perfect, shapely legs. Between the dreamy scene—the sunset, the ocean, the ritzy yacht—and the buzz she was feeling, Tiphani was mesmerized. Flashes of her kids' faces played in her mind. She couldn't help but wonder if she'd done the right thing by letting Scar stage her kidnapping.

When Scar's little henchmen had snatched her from in front of her home, they had blindfolded her and put her in a van. Tiphani, not knowing it was a set-up, had fought ferociously, clawing hunks of skin from one of their faces, kicking and biting wildly. Scar had instructed them not to hurt a hair on her head, but she didn't make it easy, cursing, spitting, and bucking like a wild animal.

After she had finally worn herself out and sat still for five minutes, Scar's men tried to explain to her what was going on, but she wouldn't hear anything from them. In her mind she had been thrust into a fight to save her own life. Only after they'd told her what Scar had instructed them to say did she listen. She was informed that Scar had ordered the fake kidnapping, just in case neighbors or any other witnesses had been watching, and that there was a reason for everything. They also told her that Scar just really wanted her to meet with him and lay low for a while.

With all of the commotion, Tiphani was trying to make sense of it all. To her it seemed to be a bit much. She thought he could've just told her to come and disappear with him without all of the theatrics, but she figured Scar knew what he was doing. They explained that Scar knew when she didn't show up for her kids, her disappearance would be reported, and everyone would think she was missing. Scar had staged the kidnapping because he wanted it to seem like she was snatched, that it had something to do with her husband's dirty dealings.

After getting wind of the meeting between his brother Derek and his old crew member Flip, it wasn't lost on Scar that Flip had probably revealed a bunch of shit that could send Scar to prison for a long time. Which was why he had to shut Flip up permanently. He'd ordered the hit to take place publicly, to send a message to anyone else who had an idea to "flip" on Scar and the Dirty Money Crew. The execution outside of the hotel definitely got everyone's attention. Word spread instantly about the fate of Flip, the snitch. Scar also knew that his brother Derek would be looking for a way to defend himself against all the charges thrown his way, which meant Derek would also be gunning for him. He knew it wouldn't be that long before the beast amassed enough evidence to finally make the charges stick.

Tiphani had protested Scar's staged kidnapping for the first couple of days, pouting and begging to go home to her kids. She was having trouble understanding the reasoning and desperately missed her kids. Knowing Scar was dangerous, she didn't push the issue as much as she wanted to. So, even though her kidnapping was supposed to be fake, she really did feel like she'd been kidnapped and was being held against her will.

Legally, she didn't think her disappearance would bring any value to the case against Derek, and she knew her kids were at risk of being forced into the foster care system in her absence. She'd even thought about Derek winning their custody battle, if he ever beat his case.

But Tiphani's protests and pleas fell on deaf ears. Scar used his charm and his dick to convince her that this staged kidnapping was the only way to put another brick in the wall against Derek. Ultimately, the dick had finally made Tiphani give in to Scar's plan. When his goons delivered Tiphani to Scar, he grabbed her and hugged her tightly. He was still playing the role of concerned lover, even though he just wanted to keep her close and keep an eye on her.

Staging the kidnap worked to Scar's advantage in two ways. One, he could make it look like Derek had something to do with it, and two, he could control Tiphani, while getting some of that tasty pussy.

After his welcoming hug, he led her down the pier, toward a line of huge yachts. Tiphani was confused, looking around in disbelief. She kept walking with Scar until he stopped in front of one of the massive boats. She read the hand-painted sign on the back of the yacht. It read "DIRTY MONEY." She looked up at Scar with furrowed eyebrows.

"I ain't gonna fake kidnap you and keep you in my basement, baby," Scar had said, smiling. He led her up the dock ramp into the boat.

Tiphani remembered her heart skipping a beat. She had quickly forgotten about her reservations about staging her own kidnapping. Scar welcomed her onto the regal boat. Inside Tiphani looked around in awe. It looked like a house. He led her into the fully furnished suite, which made her gasp. All of the furniture was pure white, and it immediately made Tiphani think about the way she envisioned Heaven. There was a California king-sized bed, leather couches, plasma TVs, expensive throw rugs, mirrored walls and ceilings, and a Jacuzzi.

Tiphani was overwhelmed by the yacht. The luxuriousness made it feel like all of her worries had dissipated right then and there. She couldn't contain herself and had to let Scar fuck her right there on the spot.

After two days on the yacht, Scar thought it was time to put Tiphani onto his full plan and get her to buy in. When he told her they'd be gone for six months or longer, she cried, thinking about her kids.

Scar's plan was for her to go back to Baltimore, act as if she had been kidnapped because of Derek, and fake like she had fought to make a daring escape. Scar told her she could sell her story to every news program—*20/20*; *Dateline*; CNN; Anderson Cooper. Shit, even *Oprah*. They would all be fighting to cover the highly publicized reunion with her kids.

Knowing the law, Tiphani didn't think getting her kids back would be that easy. She figured there would be suspicion that she'd abandoned them and made up her story, which worried her immensely. She didn't think the whole thing was a good idea.

Scar reassured her he would pay whoever he had to pay to have her kids returned to her. He also told her she should always say that her captors kept mentioning her husband, and money he owed them. If she stuck to the story, it would make it seem as if Derek was the cause of her disappearance because he had been robbing drug dealers and selling drugs too.

The best part of the plan was, while she rode the wave of fame and notoriety, she would jump out of the box and announce her bid to run for circuit court judge. Scar told her that he had it all mapped out, and she would definitely win. In his grand scheme, Tiphani would be the one that would save him from all of the charges pending against him once and for all. A lot of pockets would be laced so that she would be appointed as the judge on his case when he finally turned himself in.

Being the driven, power-hungry career woman she was, at first Tiphani thought the plan was brilliant. She could sacrifice a few months without her kids for a greater career move. In her mind, becoming a judge would be great for all of them. But she didn't know Scar would never really be loyal to anyone, not even her.

Today, sitting on a yacht with a dangerous drug dealer, Tiphani was having second thoughts. The what-ifs had set in on her, and she sat, preoccupied with thoughts of all of the things that could go wrong—one of which was, she could be thrown in jail for fabricating a story so elaborate and would lose her children forever if anyone ever found out the truth.

"Damn! You been daydreaming for a minute," Scar said, breaking up her thoughts.

Tiphani let a weak smile spread across her face.

Scar could see the second thoughts and doubt in her eyes. "I hope you dreaming about me and this pussy-pounding I'm about to put on you." He grabbed his dick through his pants.

Tiphani smiled just thinking about that good-ass dick.

When Scar saw her smile, he knew he had her again. He didn't care if he had to fuck her every minute of every day to keep her on course with his plan. He was going to do whatever it took to keep this bitch in line. Scar thought of Tiphani as the "queen of sorts." He saw her as one of the most powerful pieces in his game of chess against Derek and the Maryland State Troopers that had tried to destroy everything he had worked to build.

Before she knew it, Scar had swooped down on

her like an eagle snatching up a little mouse as prey. The next thing she knew, Scar was carrying her like a little rag doll down the yacht steps to the lower deck. Once there, he reached under her dress and ripped her thong off with one forceful motion.

Tiphani began breathing hard, and a hot feeling came over her. She loved Scar's spontaneity. Nothing was all planned and boring, like with Derek. She giggled, the liquor tingling her senses. Scar forced his tongue into her mouth, she accepted, and they kissed wildly. Tiphani's cheeks were on fire. The heat their bodies generated was enough to cook something.

Scar pulled off his Ralph Lauren purple label shorts, freeing his beautiful, thick dick. Then he ripped his wife-beater over his head, exposing his chest, adorned by a diamond-encrusted Jesus piece. The platinum up against his ebony skin was sexy as hell. Tiphani licked her lips as he climbed on top of her. She buried her face in his neck and inhaled his scent. It was intoxicating. She felt like she was really falling in love with him.

Scar hoisted her sundress up and buried his face in her sopping wet pussy. He blew his hot breath on her clitoris and devoured her pussy until she was dizzy. Then he moved up, took a mouthful of her firm breasts into his mouth, and slammed his dick up in her like a bulldozer. Over and over again, Scar pounded into her flesh. Tiphani dug her nails into his back as he continued his mission. He rammed her with all his might and fucked her back into submission.

Tiphani accepted each of his thrusts for as long as she could. "Oh God!" she screamed, and then she came all over his dick.

Then Scar followed her, letting his juices saturate her neatly shaved triangle. Panting and out of breath, they collapsed in a tangled heap of flesh.

Just then Scar's cell phone rang. "Damn!" he panted. It was back to business just that fast. Although his ass was on a vacation of sorts, shit in the harsh streets of Baltimore was business as usual.

Scar still had a strong hold on the streets through his Dirty Money Crew, which was thriving and growing in numbers. He had groomed his little niggas well, and they were running shit back home, keeping his pockets laced. Niggas was hungry on the streets, and he was the only nigga offering to feed them, so they all remained loyal to him. Even in his absence, his presence was still felt.

"Speak," he wolfed into his cell phone. He listened for a minute. Then he sat up and pushed Tiphani away, turning his back toward her. Scar flexed his jaw as he listened intently. He balled up his fist on his free hand and squeezed it so hard, his knuckles looked like they'd bust through his skin. He pursed his lips and spoke. "Well, then kill the nigga. What you even second-guessing it for?" Disconnecting the line, he tossed his cell phone across the room, sending it crashing into the wall.

Tiphani jumped at the sound. "What's the matter, baby?" she asked, sitting up startled.

Scar ignored her question. He rushed out of the room to get his anger under control. He didn't want to unleash on Tiphani and risk having her fall out of line.

Tiphani lay back down, still hoping this plan was going to work in their favor.

Chapter 2

Business as Usual

"Yo, he said to kill this nigga," Trail said, no emotion behind his words as he hung up the phone.

"No. Please, Trail, help me, man. Sticks, please," the boy pleaded as he sat on a small chair in the middle of the floor, surrounded by members of the Dirty Money Crew.

The boy's begging and pleading for mercy amused the crew, who were laughing and making light of his impending doom, but he saw it as a last-ditch effort to save himself. Only fifteen, he felt he was too young to die. The day he took Scar's offer to join the crew, he'd made the worst mistake of his life, and he knew it now more than ever.

"Nigga, your trap was short seven fuckin' times in a row. Then you show up in the hood with a fuckin' brand-new-ass Escalade, paid out in cash! You can't afford that shit, nigga. You ain't move up in this game yet. Ain't nobody gonna surpass Scar's status. When you stole from that nigga and tried to floss like you was larger than him, you sealed your fate. You thought a nigga like Scar was gone, vamoose, and that you was gonna get away with having larceny in yo' heart. Well, nigga, I just got word from the king of these streets. The order has been given—you're a dead man." Sticks' face curled into a hard scowl, stiff and emotionless like stone.

"Yo, I can pay it back. It wasn't that much, I swear. I just been saving for a minute," the boy begged, shaking his legs back and forth.

All of the Dirty Money Crew members began laughing uproariously. They thought this little begging-ass boy was amusing, and they were particularly anxious to see him get his punishment, even if it meant murder. In Scar's absence the crew all looked to Sticks for their orders, and he knew he definitely had something to prove.

"Yo, now a nigga wanna cop a plea," Timber said. He was one of the new members of the crew. "Let me kill him, slow and painful like. I will cut off his eyelids so the nigga can't blink. I will remove that nigga's fingernails and toenails one by one while he watch." Timber got menacingly close to the boy's face.

Timber was a wild boy, and he was helping the Dirty Money Crew wreak havoc on the streets of Baltimore. He had relocated from Alabama to Baltimore with his mother, and it wasn't long before he got knee-deep into the streets. He had told Sticks and Trail that he got his nickname Timber because one night when he was eleven, he went out into his backyard, sawed off a tree branch and beat his stepfather to death with it for hitting on his mother. When the word spread about him to all the gangs in Alabama, they started calling him Little Timber after that, and the name stuck. (*Tim-ber!*" was what the tree cutters in Alabama called out when they cut trees down.) After Timber felt the power surge from his first murder, it became nothing for him. He was ruthless and was into torture. In fact, he craved the sensational rush he got from committing heinous acts.

"Nah, I'ma do this shit Scar-style—short and sweet, no need for a bunch of blood and guts and shit," Sticks said. He really just wanted to assert his power and show off his bravado in front of the younger dudes in the crew. Murder and mayhem was what he wanted on his tombstone.

"Yo, Scar always gives a nigga his chance to have last rites. "So what is it gonna be?" Sticks said to the boy. You got a choice, nigga—call a bitch, call your moms, or you wanna chance to pray to God? Don't think too long, nigga. I ain't got all day."

Staring death in the eyes, the boy thought to himself, *This can't be real.* Crying like a baby and trembling like a leaf, he agreed to a call to his mother to say good-bye. He figured at least she would know he was thinking of her before he died. He couldn't imagine how she would react if he had gone missing for weeks, or when the police finally came to the door to tell her they had found his body. He wanted to tell her good-bye himself. In his mind, he was saying, *Fuck God*, because if there was a God, He would save him right now.

"I'ma call my moms," the boy whined through the tsunami of tears that covered his face.

Sticks kept his gun trained on the boy. "Tell this nigga the number to dial," he instructed the boy. The boy did as he was told, and Trail punched the numbers in on one of their many disposable track phones they used to communicate about their business and to speak to Scar, to avoid being traced.

Trail put the phone on speaker, and after three rings, the boy heard his mother's melodic voice filter through the speaker.

"Hello?" she answered.

"Ma! Ma!" the boy cried out.

"Anthony? What's the matter? Where are you?" his mother said, concern streaming through her words.

"Say bye, nigga," Sticks whispered, placing the cold steel up against the boy's temple.

"Bye, ma! I love you forever!!" the boy screamed.

"Anthony!" his mother screamed.

Trail disconnected the line.

Bang! One shot to the temple, and the boy's body slumped from the chair and hit the floor with an ominous thud.

"One down, two more Frank Lucas snitch-ass niggas to go," Sticks said. Temporarily put in charge by Scar, Sticks had vowed that the streets would be sorry for the day he was born. He remembered all the ill-treatment he'd suffered at Scar's hands in the training phase of his come-up. Now he was prepared to take it out on anybody who got in his way, even members of the crew.

Sticks, Trail, Timber, and four new young members

of the Dirty Money Crew loaded into two black Suburbans. Sticks drove slowly through the streets of Baltimore, blasting Drake and Lil Wayne. The bass and the lyrics had them all hyped. All except Sticks, who was silent and intently focused on his mission, while the other members were laughing and cracking jokes on each other.

"Yo! Y'all gotta shut the fuck up!" Sticks screamed. "We about to go handle some serious business. If Scar was here, y'all niggas would be like church mice up in this bitch, scared to fuckin' make a peep!"

An immediate hush fell over the vehicle.

"Now, we gonna ride out slow and easy. This nigga Bam think shit is one hun'ed. I wanna scope out his spots first." Sticks spoke calmly, as if he didn't just scream on them. He was a perfectionist when it came to a mission. For him, failure wasn't an option.

Sticks was a hungry dude from day one; he'd never had shit given to him. When Scar had met him, he could tell the boy would do almost anything to put food in his starving stomach. Which was why Scar had chosen him. Scar had groomed him much like a trainer would groom a prize fighter. So when Sticks collected his first couple of stacks, his loyalty to Scar was sealed. Scar figured he was the perfect one to run shit, allowing him to lay low.

They drove down a block and were careful to stay two or three buildings away from their destination.

"Look, there go that nigga right there," Trail said in a low tone, pointing out a hustler named Bam that had been on the crew's radar for some prime real estate he owned in the Baltimore drug trade.

Before anybody else could do or say anything, Sticks accelerated and rolled up on the rival dealer without warning. The truck tires screeched against the street, startling everyone on the block.

Before anyone could react, Sticks threw the truck in park and was out in a millisecond. He ran up to Bam, his gun drawn. "Yo, I thought I told you we staging a takeover of this set!" Sticks screamed as he rushed towards Bam.

Bam threw his hands up in surrender.

It was too late. He had been caught slippin' and clearly not prepared for the huge .45-caliber gun sitting in his face. "Your choice was to get down or lay down, like that dude Beanie Sigel said. You chose to lay down, muthafucka," Sticks growled.

Boom!

One shot to the dome, and Bam's body crumpled to the ground, leaving the other members of Scar's crew in shock. Screams erupted everywhere.

"Go in the mu'fucka and clean it out. Drugs and money!" Sticks barked, whirling around with his gun, swinging to ward off everybody.

The rest of the crew members raced into Bam's trap house and looted as fast as they could.

Sticks had always instructed them that they had eight minutes from beginning to end to do a "jux." He had timed the 9-1-1 response, the time it took the police to get up and out on a call.

He looked at his watch. They were almost on schedule but not quite. He could hear the distant wail of sirens. "Let's go!" he ordered. "We ain't got no witnesses." He called out to the crowd of onlookers and to Bam's little crew. "I saw all y'all faces—Anybody snitch, I will be back!"

Sticks and the rest of the Dirty Money Crew loaded back into their vehicles and rolled out.

Trail was fuming mad. He didn't understand why Sticks didn't give him any forewarning that he was going to murder Bam. He huffed, "Nigga, how you just gonna jump the fuck out and not say shit? No heads-up or nothing?"

"Hesitation leads to reservations. One ounce of doubt and you a fuckin' dead man on these streets," Sticks said calmly. He didn't give a fuck about anyone's feelings. This game and all its little quirks was all about a paper chase and power for him.

"You could've still said something," Trail told him. "Let a nigga know what you was about to do and shit."

"Damn, mu'fucka! Pull your skirt down. I can't take no bitchy whining and complaining shit. If we gonna be on this new shit, taking down all the other niggas in Baltimore, we don't have time to run our mouths like bitches. Now drop the fuckin' subject and follow my lead, nigga. I mean, you either get down or lay down!"

Trail did as he was told and shut his mouth, but he didn't like it. He twisted his lips to the side and bopped his head to the music in an effort to keep himself quiet. Shit was definitely different than when Scar was home. Trail noticed that since Scar had left, Sticks was more ruthless than ever. He was letting the young'uns run wild in the streets of Baltimore, killing any person— man, woman, or child—that got in their way. They were collecting money almost every hour. All of the street contracts and territorial agreements Scar had made with rival hustlers was out the window once he left. Sticks had single-handedly dismantled a commission of hustlers that Scar had put together years ago to divide up the drug territories and put an end to a war that was going on at the time. Although Scar had assigned himself the most lucrative spots and the biggest piece of the pie, the other hustlers got down with the commission because they were afraid of the consequences if they refused. Shit on the streets was all good after that. There were a little jealous spats here and there, but whenever niggas heard Scar wasn't happy, those little sidebar fights quickly turned into truces.

Now, Trail was worried that Sticks, if he wasn't careful, could start one of the biggest drug wars in Baltimore's history, even bigger than the one Scar put an end to where seventy street dudes had been killed in a five-month span.

Finally, Sticks pulled the vehicle up on the other side of town. Trail bit down into his jaw. He knew that this entire south side belonged to Tango, another big hustler in Baltimore. Tango and Scar had finally settled their beef over streets years ago with the formulation of the commission, drawing imaginary lines in the Baltimore streets.

"Yo, Timber, you ready to earn your wings, nigga?" Sticks asked.

"I was born ready. Where they at?" Timber said with his thick country accent.

"That's their main hub right there. I heard they

collect like six hundred thousand stacks every eight hours. We about to take their day's work." Sticks laughed like he was a damn maniac.

"A'ight, let's get it," Timber said, pulling on the truck's door handle with one hand, while he gripped a stolen AK-47 in the other.

Danielle rolled her eyes as her mother rambled on with another lecture. She was thinking, her mother just didn't get it. The more Dana told her to stay away from boys, sex, and drugs, the more Danielle was drawn to them. Today though, it was a different lecture. Her mother was trying to convince her to go and spend more time with her older sister. Ever since she had turned sixteen, Danielle had begun to smell herself, thinking she was grown.

"Why should I go spend the weekends at her house, Ma? She's a cop, and I hate the police! " Danielle said. "Plus, she's boring. Ain't nobody trying to sit up in her face all day talking about nothing at all." She folded her arms across her ample breasts and shifted her weight from one foot to another.

Dana was determined to get her to focus on something other than the streets and she wasn't trying to hear it. "First of all, your sister has a very good job. She helps pay most of the bills in here and keeps you in all of that expensive stuff you like to wear. You can show her you appreciate her. She loves you, and besides, you used to like to spend time with her."

Danielle rolled her eyes as she applied a full face of make-up. At sixteen, she resembled a grown-ass woman. Thirty-six D cup breasts, a small waist, plump round hips, and an ass you could set a glass on made her a hot commodity in the hood. She got a million attempts at getting with her a day, and knew just how to play the game. Danielle wasn't interested in traditional school. She was from the "use-what-you-got-to-get-what-you-want" school, having learned from the best—her mother. And she damn sure didn't have time to spend with her lame-ass sister.

"Look, you're becoming too spoiled, Dani. One day your sister is going to cut you off, and then what you gon' do? Huh?" Her mother took a long drag off her cigarette.

Danielle sucked her teeth. She always felt unloved because she never knew her father. And ever since she could remember, Maria had been like a second parent.

"Fine. I'll go with her for the weekend, if you let me go to a party with Veronica and my friends first."

"She will be here on Saturday morning to get you, so have your ass back up in here. You act like spending time with her is going to kill you. You should try to appease her, as much as she does for us. When she cuts us off, your lips gonna be poked out. If that happens, your hot ass ain't gonna get those little stripper-ass outfits you like to wear." Dana blew a ring of smoke toward her daughter.

"Whatever. I'll be here. Yeah, sure," Danielle said, grabbing her purse and heading out the door.

Danielle rushed up the street, switching her hips as hard as she could. She smirked to herself at all of the catcalls she received from the little hood-rat dudes in her neighborhood.

"Yo, Dani, I will fuck those poom-poom shorts right off that fat ass," a little corner boy called out.

"Nigga, *pa-lease*! I fucks with real hustlers. Hand-to-hand is played out!" Danielle screamed, craning her neck in true ghetto-girl fashion.

She finally made it to the end of the block, where she spotted the person she was expecting to meet. Her heart jumped in her chest. He was so damn sexy. Danielle let a smile spread across her face at the sight of the gleaming silver Benz S550 he sat in. She rushed over to the passenger side and slid in.

"Damn, baby girl! You got my shit on wood with them li'l shorts," Sticks said, licking his lips. *I have something for this little hottie*, he thought to himself.

"Two weeks and you can't handle seeing me in shorts?" She leaned over to kiss her new man.

Everybody in Baltimore knew Sticks was down with the Dirty Money Crew, including Danielle and her little friends. But she was so excited when Sticks had stopped her in a party. In fact she felt extra special that he had chosen her out of all the girls in the club that night. Sticks had told her she reminded him of Lauren London, a comment she got all the time, but coming from him, it made her blush.

That night Danielle gave Sticks her number. Her best friend Veronica had stayed up with her all night waiting for him to call, but he never did. Three days had passed, and Danielle had gotten a little depressed. Then, when she least expected it, Sticks showed up at her high school. It just so happened, that day she'd decided to attend classes. She'd rolled her eyes at him and told him off.

Sticks laughed at her and told her he liked the way she looked when she was mad. He grabbed her hand and led her to his car. He started calling her every day since.

"Where you wanna go, mami? The world is yours," Sticks said, tossing a money stack into her lap.

Danielle's eyes lit up. She didn't want to seem too thirsty by picking up the stack and counting it, but she wanted to so badly. "I wanna be wherever you are. We could sit in this car all night and I'd be happy," she replied.

That's exactly what Sticks wanted to hear. He liked the little pretty girl, but he also had bigger plans for her. Before he put her to work, he wanted to run up in that fat ass. He took her to get something to eat at Ruth's Chris, one of his favorites.

Danielle had never been to a real restaurant like that. The closest she'd come was when her sister had taken them out to eat at the local Olive Garden.

"Thank you for dinner, baby. I really appreciate everything you do for me." Danielle smiled, causing her deep dimples to show.

"Yo, ma, you know I keep it one hun'ed, right?" Sticks asked, his tone serious.

"Yes. Why? What's the matter?"

"I want you, ma. I know I said I wanted to wait until you was seventeen and shit, but I think a nigga fallin' for you."

"Ohhh, Sticks, I already fell for you," Danielle said, leaning over into the driver's seat so she could kiss him.

"Come home with me."

"Okay. Anything for you." Danielle had never felt the warm feeling she was feeling inside right now. *It must be love*, she thought.

Sticks knew as soon as he gave Danielle a taste of the dick, her young mind would be his to mold.

He and Danielle entered the doors to his luxury condo wrapped together. They were in a tangle of arms and legs, kissing and licking each other hot and heavy.

Danielle straddled Sticks around the waist, and he held onto her plump ass. As Sticks carried her up the stairs toward the bedroom in a rush, they thrust their tongues down each other's throats. Her breathing was labored, her heart hammering against her chest bone, and her ears were ringing, she was so excited. See, Danielle had only had sex with two other guys, and they were young boys, so she was scared to death.

Sticks lay her on the bed and started kissing her bare butter-colored thighs. Her shorts were hitched up so far into her crotch, she had a serious camel toe. The sight turned Sticks on immensely.

Danielle's thighs trembled. No matter how hard she tried to control her nerves, she couldn't. Sticks licked down her thighs to her calves. Then he lifted one of her legs and licked behind her knee, sending needle pricks all over her body.

"Mmmm," she moaned.

Like an expert, Sticks stealthily removed her shorts before she even knew what had happened. He stared down at her young, fresh, pink, unblemished flesh. "That's a pretty pussy," he grunted as he slid his hands up her shirt and pulled it over her head. He unsnapped her bra with one hand as he kissed her deep.

Danielle felt so hot, she thought she would explode. She didn't know what to expect, but she knew she wanted it badly. She just wanted Sticks to keep touching her and taking her.

When Danielle was fully naked, Sticks got off the bed and stood up to look at her. He stared at her like she was a fine meal that he was about to devour.

Danielle had her eyes closed. When she didn't feel him anymore, she opened them. "What's the matter?" she asked, closing her legs.

"Nothing, ma. I just wanted to admire your beauty. You are really gorgeous." Sticks didn't tell many chicks they were gorgeous, but Danielle really was. Her skin was smooth and seemingly untouched. He thought she looked so pure, unlike some of the scarred-up, sagging-tit chicks he fucked with normally.

Sticks removed his clothes and climbed back onto the bed. He placed his mouth over hers, and they kissed again. This time it wasn't wild and lustful, but slow and steady. It made Danielle feel loved.

While he kissed her, Sticks used his knee to part her trembling legs. He grabbed his rock-hard dick and guided it to her flesh, making Danielle jump.

"I'm not gonna hurt you," he said. Then he gently entered her.

"Aghhh!" she gasped. A sharp pain shot through her pelvis.

Sticks moved in and out of her slowly at first. His eyes popped open from the feeling he got from her body. He was shocked. He didn't expect her pussy to be so tight. She really felt like a virgin. Sticks was even more enamored with her now.

"Aghhh, aghhh!" Danielle grunted, biting down into her lip.

The sounds of her moans, and the suction Sticks felt from her tight walls made his head spin. He pulled out of her to keep himself from busting a nut.

"C'mere," he whispered. After pulling Danielle up off the bed, he lay down and guided her on top of him.

She straddled him and sat down on his dick. "Aghhh!" she screamed out from the pain. Paralyzed with pain, she wasn't ready to take all of his thick, long tool.

Sticks grabbed onto her hips and guided her up and down on him, until she started feeling more pleasure than pain. "That's it, ma. Slow and steady. You like this dick, or you love it?"

"I love it!!" Danielle screamed. "I love you!!"

Sticks didn't return the four-letter word, but he was damn sure glad she had said it. He could feel the nut welling up inside of him. He began pumping his hips, causing Danielle to bounce up and down. Her titties bouncing in his face was turning him on even more. He lifted his head slightly and took a mouthful of one of her nipples.

"Oh, yes!" she screamed.

Sticks sucked hard and fucked her even harder. He felt it welling up. He moved faster. Faster.

"Aghhhh! I feel something!" Danielle hollered. She had never had an orgasm. The feeling busting through her loins made her pump on the dick even harder and faster. She didn't feel pain anymore, just pure, hot, wet pleasure.

"Uggghhh!" Sticks growled, his body stiffening and jerking as he released his hot load.

Danielle felt his liquid dripping back out of her. She was too hot and too in love to think about any consequences. "Oh my God," Danielle cried, and she lay on top of Sticks' perfect chest.

Sticks was silent, his usual manner when thinking hard. He couldn't believe this little, inexperienced girl wound up giving him the best sex he'd ever had.

Chapter 3

Sealed Fate

Derek felt like he had eaten a jar of paste. His mouth was dry, and his throat ached. He swallowed hard, trying to fight his nerves as the court officers led him into the courtroom. He had almost shit on himself when his lawyer came to the court cells earlier that day to tell him that the jury had reached a verdict in his trial. Derek knew a fast verdict like that could go either way, for conviction or acquittal. He could only pray that the jury was made up of reasonable citizens who would take into account his service to the community and city of Baltimore.

As he was led in, Derek saw Archie's whole family seated in the front of the courtroom. His wife, kids, and parents were all there waiting to see justice being served. Derek's heart jerked in his chest. He still couldn't believe everyone would actually think he had something to do with Archie's murder. Derek was an usher in Archie's wedding; he'd brought the entire DES hand-rolled cigars when Archie had his first baby. He thought it was just crazy that none of those facts was allowed to be brought out during the trial. Instead, the prosecutor's office had made Derek out to be a demon who killed to cover up his misdeeds, painting him as a lowlife that worked for the very criminals he was supposed to be putting away.

Although Derek had gotten into some dirty shit with Scar, he would never kill one of his own men. No one knew the reason he worked with Scar. Scar was his baby brother. Derek normally hated drug dealers and what they stood for, but he'd made a promise to his mother to always take care of Scar. He had taken that promise to heart, and now it had landed him in hell.

Embarrassed, nervous, and angry, Derek averted eye contact with any of the other Maryland state troopers in the courtroom, including Chief Hill and Rodriguez. The walk to his seat felt like an eternity. He took his spot behind the defense table and sat down. The lights in the courtroom felt super bright, as if a huge stage spotlight was shining right on him. The air in the courtroom seemed so thick and stale, Derek felt like he'd suffocate. To get some relief, he adjusted his tie to get some air.

Derek couldn't help but think the worst. He was going to jail for life. He said a silent prayer. He could feel sweat sliding down his forehead, dampening the underarms of his shirt. As the news cameras rolled, he swore he could feel the heat of the entire world's eyes on him through the camera lenses. He was usually cool under pressure, but at this moment he thought he was about to lose it completely. The tension was too much. He wasn't sure he would be able to handle life in prison, especially for something he wasn't guilty of. His fate was in the hands of the jury now.

"All rise. The Honorable Judge Irvin Klein presiding," the court officer called out.

The sound of wood creaking and bodies shifting seemed unnervingly loud to Derek as everyone in the courtroom stood up. Once the judge was behind the bench, everyone took their seats again.

"Remain standing, Mr. Fuller," Judge Klein instructed. "We might as well get this over with as quickly as possible."

Derek felt his legs weaken then buckle. He took a deep breath to try and calm his nerves, which didn't work.

"Jury, have you reached a verdict in the matter of the State of Maryland versus Mr. Derek Fuller?" the judge asked.

A sickening hush fell over the room, and Derek's stomach let out a loud growl. He had nervous bowel syndrome. He hunched over slightly, which was all he could do to keep himself from throwing up or shitting on himself.

"We have, Your Honor." The jury foreman, a rail-thin white man who'd been a military police officer, stood up slowly.

Derek's defense attorney had tried to dismiss the man during voir dire, arguing that he would be prejudiced and overly sensitive to a police murder, but the prosecutor had fought to keep him and won.

"Jury, what say you?" Judge Klein asked, looking over the edge of his wire-rimmed glasses at Derek.

"As to count one of the indictment, murder in the first degree, we the jury find the defendant guilty," the foreman read.

Derek's legs buckled, and he fell back into the hardwood chair.

The courtroom erupted in pandemonium. Cameras zoomed into Derek's face as he sat there in shock. His worst nightmare had come true. Archie's wife cried out in part joy and part agony, while other officers in the room began cheering and jeering.

The court officers rushed over to Derek and grabbed him up out of the chair. At first he put up no fight, but then, suddenly, flashes of anger sparked through him. He knew he didn't stand a chance at sentencing.

"I gave my life for this fucking city! I am a cop and this is how you mu'fuckas repay me? I was the one who gave the DA details about Scar Johnson! I'm innocent, you bastards! Can't you see this is a set-up? I didn't kill Archie! I didn't kill anyone!!" Derek screamed as the court officers manhandled him, thrashing against their grasp violently. He wasn't going down without a fight. "You all will regret this shit! I'm fucking innocent!"

The court officers finally got him into a tight arm bar and forcefully removed him from the courtroom, but Derek continued his rant, which fell on deaf ears. The entire city of Baltimore had pegged him as a cop killer.

Chief Hill smiled and gave Rodriguez a pat on her back. "I guess you did it," he said, chuckling a little.

A pang of guilt flitted through Rodriguez's stomach. She knew, without the evidence she had planted, Derek's attorney would have been able to establish reasonable doubt in the case. She hung her head in shame. Here it is, one of her fellow officers was just falsely convicted of killing one of his peers, and their fucking chief was celebrating. The department was being racked with corruption and disloyalty, and she didn't know who to trust anymore. She really believed some criminals were more loyal than some cops.

When Chief Hill had threatened to blackmail her, Rodriguez got a harsh reality check that every cop had a price, that in Baltimore, dirty justice was up for sale to the highest bidder.

Thinking about the money, Rodriguez looked down at her Bulova watch. She had to meet up with one of Scar's workers for her final payment. Part of her agreement with Scar was, if Derek was convicted, she would get an extra fifty thousand dollars. Yes, she felt bad about Derek getting convicted, but she still felt like she needed to look out for number one. She damn sure wasn't about to turn down an extra fifty grand because Derek pissed off the wrong people. Rodriguez just figured she played the game better than he did, and she wasn't about to try and change a system that had been in place for years before she came around and would still be in place after she left. But after this she was done. The guilt she felt wasn't worth the money. She had enough and was ready to get out of the corruption game. She told herself that after she collected the money she would not play on Scar's team anymore. She had other plans for her life, including trying to be a good daughter and big sister. She was the leader of her family.

Rodriguez rushed out of the courthouse. She wanted to pick up her loot and then go pick up Danielle. *Maybe I'll take her shopping to celebrate,* she thought.

Rodriguez definitely knew a little something about the hard-knock life. When their mother had escaped their abusive father and ran to Maryland from New York, all she had was her children and the clothes on her back. Being Puerto Rican down in the South wasn't easy. Her mother did odd jobs cleaning people's houses and waiting tables part-time, to take care of her children the best she could. The entire family was teased and ridiculed for being Hispanic, including Rodriguez, who worked little odd jobs as a kid and through high school to help her mother out. When she decided to join the police force, it was as if she had struck gold. They were used to living piss-poor, so having a stable income, no matter how modest, was better than living paycheck to paycheck from dead-end jobs.

Just thinking about the turn her life was taking made Rodriguez angry with herself. She swore that this was going to be the last crooked thing she did.

Her mind heavy, Rodriguez drove up to the new warehouse where Scar's new crew of young gunners had set up shop. She felt more comfortable coming to the deserted warehouse because it was on the outskirts of the city, and since it was a new spot for the crew, the police didn't know about it yet. So she didn't have to worry about anyone associating her with drug dealers.

She picked up her cell and sent a cryptic text to the phone number Sticks had provided her. It was a code to let Sticks know she was outside to collect her money. While waiting, she heard, *Bang! Bang!*

Rodriguez almost jumped out of her skin. Someone had banged on her car window. Inhaling deep and exhaling slow, she tried to calm the thundering in her chest. She was finally able to control her trembling hand long enough to press the window button.

"Why the hell are you sneaking up on me like that?" She touched her gun for assurance.

"I just like fucking with you, that's why," Sticks said, cracking up like he was watching the funniest comedy show. "Ay, yo!" He called out a little code he and the crew used, and suddenly the iron gate to the warehouse slowly began rising.

Rodriguez put her car in park and stepped out. As she got closer, she heard rap music blaring and could smell the weed smoke coming from inside the warehouse. There had to be about twenty guys in the warehouse. Some were at a table counting money, some were bagging drugs, while some were in different stages of sexual acts with girls. But most of them were standing guard with huge assault weapons in hand.

Rodriguez thought it was a shame the way Scar was leading the youth of Baltimore astray. Almost none of the Dirty Money Crew members were older than seventeen, because Scar knew that meant they would be charged as minors for most of the crimes they'd commit. Rodriguez felt like shit inside for being a part of the city's destruction.

"Yo, Trail, get this bitch her pay," Sticks ordered.

Trail gritted his teeth. He fucking hated that Sticks tried so hard to act like Scar, ordering him around like they hadn't started out together on the same level. Sticks was taking this stand-in role as leader to the head, and Trail was growing more and more fed up by the day. Trail walked slowly to retrieve the money.

Rodriguez looked around. She thought back to a time when she was running up in a spot like this, taking everybody to jail. She scanned the room in disbelief, and then she spotted someone, which almost made her faint. She squinted and blinked her eyes, thinking that they were deceiving her. *That can't be her,* she thought to herself.

Just then Danielle rose up from the chair and turned around. "Baby, I'm done with this stack," she yelled to Sticks. She locked eyes with Rodriguez, and she stopped breathing for a minute. Then she started coughing.

Rodriguez let an evil look take over her face as she stared at her, and Danielle quickly turned around and walked in the opposite direction of where her sister stood. She was shocked to see Rodriguez there. Rodriguez was equally shocked, but she knew she would risk putting Danielle in grave danger if she grabbed her up like she wanted to. That would give the impression that Danielle was affiliated with law enforcement and put her in harm's way. Rodriguez was fuming inside, and she couldn't stop staring at her little sister.

"See something you like over there? I didn't know you liked to lick pussy. Yeah, you look like one of them dike bitches," Sticks said.

Rodriguez snapped out of her trance. "No, I'm just admiring how you are keeping stuff together while Scar is away," Rodriguez fabricated on the spot.

Just as she said that, Trail returned with a small knapsack and threw it at her feet. "Fifty, like Scar told you," Trail said dryly, quickly turning his back and walking away.

Danielle sat down on one of the couches and looked her sister up and down. She put her head to the side and twisted her lips. *I can't believe her ass is a dirty cop. Oh, I'ma have a field day with her paper now. She gonna pay me. I betcha Mama don't know about this,* she thought to herself.

Danielle knew she could never let Sticks find out she was so closely related to Rodriguez. Being down with a cop—something she would never reveal to the crew—was a sure way to get herself killed. Especially with the big day they'd all been planning for coming up. It was going to be Danielle's chance to finally establish herself and get out from under her sister's controlling ass. After their upcoming lick, Danielle figured she would get enough money that she wouldn't have to spend time with her lame-ass sister. She would be able to support herself and buy herself all the fly shit she wanted.

Rodriguez took one last look at Danielle before she turned to leave. Danielle saw her looking, so she got up, walked over to Sticks, and began tonguing him down. She wanted her sister to know she was grown, that she was establishing her own independence.

***

Back in her car, Rodriguez slammed her hands on the steering wheel. She was livid. How could Danielle be so stupid, getting involved with a crew of criminals? She was even more mad at herself. She had sold her soul to the devil, and now the role model she tried to portray to her impressionable sister was shattered.

"She can't be involved with Scar's crew," Rodriguez mumbled to herself. "I will put a stop to this shit."

It took her a while to pull out. She kept contemplating getting out of her car, storming back into the warehouse, and snatching Danielle out of there by her hair. She could picture herself shaking her until her damn brain stem came loose. She was just that angry.

Finally, Rodriguez rationalized that it would be way too dangerous for them both, because the Dirty Money Crew weren't afraid to kill a cop. Feeling totally helpless, she pulled out and drove off. Her new mission was to save her sister before it was too late.

Watching from across the street, the person trailing Sticks witnessed the whole scenario that just played out. When Scar was in town running the Dirty Money Crew, he had a shadow trailing him and plotting to take him down. Now that he was missing in action, the shadow was now following Sticks, the apparent heir to Scar's empire. It was surprising to see Rodriguez at the warehouse. The shadow figured she would have been at the courthouse watching to see the outcome of the case against Detective Fuller.

As Rodriguez drove off, the shadow thought, *Apparently no one has any loyalty in B-More. Is anybody on the straight and narrow in this city?* Making a mental note to find out what shit Rodriguez was into, the shadow stayed put to stake out the warehouse. The main focus right now was to take down the Dirty Money Crew.

Tiphani lowered her head as she heard the news reporter's words.

"Today, former Maryland state trooper DES Detective Derek Fuller was found guilty of first-degree murder of DES officer Christian Archie. Fuller's sentencing will be held next month. The prosecutor's office is seeking the death penalty in the case."

Tiphani, torn between a whirlwind of emotions, had a frail smile on her face. She thought about her life with Derek and how hard he'd tried to please her. She felt slightly guilty and responsible for his entire downfall. Then she thought about her kids. How would she explain all of this to them? Tiphani felt horrible that they would grow up without Derek, that their only memories would be of the media reports that their father was a crooked cop and a murderer.

Tiphani closed her eyes and tried to make herself feel better. It was hard. She tried to think of negative things about Derek. Then she remembered that he'd tried to take her children from her. That was enough for the moment. She clung to that one thought because it helped ease her guilt.

She thought about the way she was going to look

in her judge's robe when she returned to Baltimore. That alone made her feel much, much better. She was finally smiling. Then she let out a small laugh. "He just got what was coming to him," she whispered. "That's all."

Tiphani looked over at Scar's sleeping form, watching him as he took each breath. She felt all dreamy inside. She sometimes couldn't believe that she was really in love with Scar. The time on the boat had proved him to be more attentive and charming than she thought he could be.

While with her, he had put aside the tough-guy exterior that he displayed on the street, doing little things for her, like rubbing her feet, or making her little animals out of paper to cheer her up when she was missing her kids. He would hold her when she cried, stroking her hair gently, and kissing the top of her head to comfort her. Tiphani felt that Scar was more than just some street thug that killed people. He was the man she was in love with. She often thought about what it would be like if she could have an open relationship with him, or if they could get married. Tiphani wanted to be with Scar all of the time for the rest of her life and could only hope he felt the same way.

Tiphani reached over and turned the TV off. She slid into the bed and eased her body behind Scar's. Then she threw her arm around him and hugged him. This was where she wanted to be forever.

Chapter 4

The Return

Six Months Later

Tiphani stumbled into the emergency room at Baltimore General Hospital. "Help! Help me!" she screamed, her eyes wide and dazed, blood dripping down her face. "Please help me!" she squealed again.

Everyone inside the bustling county hospital ER turned and stared at her. One lady put her hands over her mouth in shock.

The triage nurse jumped up and rushed toward Tiphani. "Get a team!" she yelled into a small handheld radio device.

Tiphani screamed again, "They are gonna kill me!" and then she collapsed to the floor.

A team of doctors and nurses rushed to her side. They worked together and hoisted her up off the floor onto a gurney. "She's got a large laceration on the head," the lead surgeon said to the team. "Appears to have bruising everywhere. Looks like some-body worked her over pretty good."

"Help me!" Tiphani screamed, seeming to come back alive. Clothed in only a dirty, ripped white tee-shirt, she started thrashing her bare legs wildly. Her hair was matted, her entire body bruised, and the soles of her feet were filthy like she'd walked a thou-sand miles barefoot to get there.

"Strap her down!" the doctor demanded as Tiph-ani bucked and thrashed wildly. "She appears to be going into shock!" The team rushed to strap her to the temporary bed.

Once inside the examination room, Tiphani be-gan screaming again, this time, just a high-pitched shriek.

"We need to sedate her in order to treat her," one of the nurses said.

After a nod from the doctor, the nurse skittered away to retrieve a syringe filled with a mild sedative. She plunged it into one of Tiphani's thighs, and Tiph-ani's body quickly went slack. She was knocked out.

For the next hour, the nurses and doctors exam-ined her limp body, her face riddled with bruises. Since she had no identification, the hospital staff treating her had planned to take fingerprints while she was knocked out so they could try to identify her.

Before they could get a technician to take the prints, one of the nurses looked at Tiphani closely. She crinkled her eyebrows and mumbled to herself, "This lady looks very familiar. I know I've seen her somewhere before."

She rushed out of the room and went into the ER's

lobby. She ran over to the bulletin board that displayed all of Baltimore's WANTED and MISSING posters. The nurse looked up and down at each row of pictures. "I knew it!" she screamed, snatching Tiphani's picture off the board. She ran back to Tiphani's room like she was on fire. "Doctor! Doctor!" she called out, waving the MISSING poster in front of her. "Somebody needs to call the police!"

Tiphani's eyes fluttered as she came into consciousness. She could hear voices around her. "Help," she rasped out.

Somebody moved toward her quickly. "Mrs. Fuller?" a man said. "I am Detective Hanson."

"Mmm, save me," Tiphani croaked.

"No one can hurt you now, Ms. Fuller. We will protect you," the detective said, standing at the side of Tiphani's hospital bed.

After a minute of staring at her, the detective got right to the point. "Ms. Fuller, do you know what happened to you? Who hurt you like this?"

"They hurt me. They said they would kill me. They said it was because of him," she said through tears.

"Who? Ms. Fuller, tell us who," Detective Hanson replied, his eyes sympathetic.

Detective Hanson was drawn in, and Tiphani knew it. She could tell by the concern written on his face that her Oscar-worthy performance had worked like a charm. She had everyone at the hospital fooled. Once again, Scar had steered her in the right direction. Tiphani had endured the most painful part of her role—the self-inflicted injuries—just so the entire plan would come together realistically.

Derek almost choked on his own spit when the breaking news report streamed across the TV screen and interrupted his daily dose of *The Maury Show*. The breaking news was that Tiphani had made a daring escape from her captors after six months and ran for her life right into the Baltimore County Hospital room. It was also being reported that the police were questioning Tiphani, and so far they believe her kidnapping is directly related to her husband's crimes.

Derek couldn't take anymore. He rushed into his cell, his mind racing once again. Although he was pissed off that he was being blamed once again for something he didn't do, a feeling of relief settled over him. At least his kids would not be in the system and they'd have their mother, he reasoned. Derek thought the entire kidnapping had Scar written all over it. He could only wonder if his wife would stoop so low as to be a part of it as well.

Tiphani's recovery went quickly but not quickly enough for her, as some of the scars from the injuries she and Scar inflicted on her body were still slightly visible. The day Tiphani left the hospital, she was swarmed by reporters from all over. Even the BBC wanted a piece of her. A hailstorm of questions were thrown at her as soon as she stepped through the hospital's revolving doors.

Secretly, Tiphani was loving every minute of the attention. She was one hundred percent sure the District Attorney Anthony Gill and Mayor Mathias Steele had been watching the reports on her. She stood at the podium and fielded question after question.

"I am just happy to be alive. I was held for months with little to no food. I was beaten and verbally abused," Tiphani said, her voice cracking as she acted like she was choking back tears. The crowd that had gathered was hanging on her every word.

"Although I cannot identify my abductors because they kept themselves hidden behind masks, I am sure that the police will find them and justice will be served. I have no further comments." Tiphani waited to be escorted into the black Lincoln Town Car that was waiting for her.

Tiphani's popularity soared. She was booked on every news and talk show. When Oprah's show producers called her, she'd jumped up and down when she hung up the phone. Her reunion with her kids was highly publicized as well, one reporter even commenting that the entire thing seemed "staged."

Tiphani was dubbed a heroic survivor. On every show she appeared on, she made sure to act as if she was very saddened by Derek's conviction. But she always made it a point to say that his actions had put her and her children in harm's way and that she was filing for divorce. Tiphani touted herself as an upstanding citizen on the right side of justice. She would quote the law and ensure that she appeared not only as a strong and brave victim, but also a sharp, well-versed attorney ready to take her career to the next level. She was establishing a solid platform to announce her political plans.

Tiphani appeared on *Oprah* dressed in a red two-piece skirt suit, red being the power color for female candidates running for public office. Tiphani sat up straight, folded her hands in her lap, and made sure she gave the proper amount of eye contact. She answered Oprah's questions without a hitch. She also shed a lot of fake tears when she had to speak about Derek and her so-called ordeal at the hands of people he was mixed up with. Then, without warning, she announced her plans to run for Baltimore County circuit court judge right there before millions of viewers. Even Oprah was caught a bit off guard by Tiphani's abrupt announcement. She told Oprah and the entire world that she was committed to public safety and justice, which was her reason for running for one of the circuit court judgeships. Tiphani smiled brightly when she received a standing ovation from the crowd. She could only hope Scar was watching their plan in action.

After almost two weeks of having no contact with Scar, Tiphani was going through withdrawal. She hadn't seen him since he had dropped her off a few miles from the hospital the day she'd reappeared. The night after the taping of her appearance on Oprah, Scar contacted her and told her that he would return to Baltimore as soon as she won her seat.

"I miss you so much," she cried into the phone.

Scar just listened with no response. All he had on

his mind was helping her win so that he could finally beat these cases against him and live the rest of his life in peace.

Chapter 5

Setting It Off

Danielle sat with her arms folded, her head cocked to the side as she looked across the table at her big sister Maria in disgust. The scowl on her face spoke volumes. Her older sister had been calling her and showing up at her house almost every day since she had seen her inside of the Dirty Money Crew's warehouse. Finally Danielle had agreed to meet with her because she couldn't take the pressure from their mother, and she damn sure couldn't stand her pig-ass sister blowing up her cell phone while she was with Sticks.

Danielle had decided she was there today to tell her sister that she wanted her to get the hell out of her business. She didn't need her sister sniffing around and blowing up her spot. She was loyal to Sticks, and Maria could kick rocks if she didn't understand that. At sixteen, she decided that she'd rather ride or die with Sticks, who she had fallen deeply in love with, than listen to her overbearing and overprotective sister. *This bitch thinks she's somebody's mama,* Danielle thought.

"Are you going to eat?" Maria asked softly. She could read Danielle's body language very well. It didn't take a rocket scientist to figure out that the teenage girl didn't want to be there.

"Yup. When I leave here I will eat. My man will buy me food. I don't want anything from you, including the food that you buy."

Trying to remain calm, Maria lowered her eyes and shoveled a forkful of pasta into her mouth. What she really wanted to do was reach across the table and slap the taste from her little sister's mouth.

"Why would you get involved with a crew like that? Do you really know who they are? They murder people, Danielle. Do you even know who Scar Johnson is? What he is capable of? Not only is it dangerous to be associated with people like that, it's stupid," Maria whispered harshly, letting her feelings drip through every word.

"You don't know nothing about me or them. You think you wrote the book because you're a fuckin' crooked-ass cop that takes bribes and shit!" Danielle screamed out, garnering looks from other patrons inside the restaurant. Danielle thought her sister was a big hypocrite. She was already regretting that she let her mother strong-arm her into meeting with her, knowing their mother always took her big sister's side.

"Don't worry about what I do. Do as I say, not as

I do. I am a grown-ass woman. I can handle myself. This street shit is not a game to be played by little girls." Maria gritted her teeth, squinting her eyes into slits. She figured if she was hard with her little sister, it would show her concern.

Rodriguez was truly troubled by her sister's new affiliations. They had come as a surprise. She obviously didn't know Danielle as well as she'd thought. Both sisters were stubborn as mules, so Maria knew telling Danielle what to do wouldn't work, but still she tried.

"What? Don't' tell me what to do. I'm never going to do as you say! Who the fuck are you? Don't try to play the big-sister role. This game is also not for crooked-ass cops. You don't fit in anywhere. I have one mother," Danielle barked, rolling her eyes. "I don't need you on my back."

"Danielle! I forbid you from seeing Sticks, and you also need to stay out of their warehouse. Don't you know if the police run up in there and find all of those drugs and guns, you're going to jail for a long, long time. I won't be able to help you," Rodriguez spat, feeling like it was her duty to school Danielle.

Danielle began laughing. "Look, stupid, how many ways I gotta say it? Sticks is my man. Read my lips— I . . . love . . . him. You can't stop that. Now after sixteen years you think you can tell me what to do and who to see? Well, you can't!" Danielle screamed. "Why don't you just fuck off and leave me alone!" She pushed her chair back so hard, it hit the floor.

Everyone in the restaurant was watching and whispering about them now. Rodriguez tried to smile weakly to get the attention off of them, but it was too late. She and the onlookers watched as Danielle stormed out of the restaurant.

Danielle walked a few yards and suddenly felt physically sick. Her sister had aggravated her so much, her stomach started cramping. She felt a flash of heat come over her entire body then an overwhelming wave of nausea hit her like a Mack truck. She hunched over and threw up. She was hurling her brains out. When the entire contents of her stomach was out on the ground, she stood upright and tried to be strong on her weak legs, wiping her mouth and inhaling in an effort to get herself together.

Just then her phone began vibrating. She snatched it out of her bag; she wasn't in the mood for her sister or her mother. She looked at the screen and saw that it was Sticks calling. "Fuck!" she cursed under her breath. Her heart almost skipped a beat with fear. She knew if she answered it, he would ask where she was, and he'd probably say he was coming to get her.

Danielle started thinking quick about what she would say. Not wanting to be associated with Rodriguez at all, there was no way she could tell Sticks she was at a restaurant with her sister. She also couldn't risk lying to Sticks and saying she was in school because she never knew when he would show up. Unable to think of a lie quick enough, she decided to ignore Sticks' call. She figured she would get her head together and then call him back when she was calm and had thought out her lie.

Immediately Danielle dialed Veronica's number, the only other person Sticks found acceptable for her to hang out with. Sticks had forced her to cut off ties with all her other friends, both male and female. She nervously shifted her weight from one foot to the other as she waited for Veronica to pick up her phone. If Sticks was looking for her and couldn't find her, it wouldn't be long before he started scouring the streets.

After what seemed like an eternity, her friend answered, and a feeling of relief washed over her.

"Veronica, I need you to come get me. I'm downtown, and Sticks is already looking for me. I was with my lame-ass sister, and now I won't be able to explain to him where I was at. Get your ass here as soon as possible," Danielle said nervously. She was so focused on her phone call, she didn't notice she was being watched.

After paying the bill, Rodriguez came outside. She was surprised to see her sister still standing out there. Trying to seize the opportunity, she rushed over to Danielle and tried again in vain to speak with her.

Not wanting anything else to do with her sister, Danielle began to walk away. Getting the hint, Rodriguez extended an envelope to her, which stopped Danielle in her tracks. Danielle knew it was the money for her mother. The money was the whole purpose of her meeting with her sister. Danielle may have been pissed off at her sister, but she wasn't about to mess with her mother's money. Reluctantly she snatched the envelope and threw it into her pocketbook.

Neither sister spoke. Danielle had more pressing issues to take care of, namely, how she was going to lie to Sticks.

Maria was too stubborn and knew she was wasting her breath, so she walked away feeling dejected.

"What the fuck is this bitch doing meeting with a fucking cop? Ain't this about a bitch? She is probably a fucking snitch! That's why that mu'fucka was staring at her the other day," Sticks mumbled to himself.

Sticks had seen enough. He gripped the steering wheel of his car, willing himself not to get out and just shoot Danielle in the head right then and there. He had watched her go into the restaurant, with Rodriguez following right behind. At first, he figured it must've been a crazy coincidence, but then he remembered the way Rodriguez was staring at Danielle at the warehouse like she knew her. When Danielle came out alone, Sticks figured they'd planned it that way, just in case anyone was watching. But seeing her take the envelope from the cop was all he needed to draw a conclusion. That was how snitches rolled. He was really convinced she was a snitch when he saw her throwing up. *She sick because she is nervous as hell. I got something for that bitch. Can't believe I fell in love with this traitor-ass bitch,* he thought to himself as he watched the first girl he'd ever loved betray him.

Sticks wasn't the only one doing surveillance at the restaurant. The Shadow, like always, was there following Sticks. Since Scar's disappearance, the Shadow had been constantly trailing Sticks. In his inexperience, Sticks didn't even for a second think about anyone following him. He was starting to feel invincible in his new role as unofficial leader of the Dirty Money Crew.

All the same, this current situation was confusing to the Shadow. Why did the cop from the warehouse hand an envelope to Sticks' woman? What was the connection? It was getting hard for him to figure out all the different players and side deals going on in the Dirty Money Crew. He started thinking there was only so much information he could gather from the outside, that it might be time to infiltrate the crew, start taking them down from the inside. *It's time to join the Dirty Money Crew*, the Shadow thought. *But how?*

Not knowing how to handle the situation, Rodriguez sat inside her car for a little while. Her conscience was eating at her as she thought about losing Danielle to the streets. She blamed herself. *Maybe if I was a better sister she wouldn't need to be in the streets. Maybe I should've never gotten down with Scar's crew and betrayed Derek.* All of these thoughts ran through her mind one after the other, like an electronic billboard sign.

Rodriguez closed her eyes to try and stop the images from scrolling. She had to admit that she knew all along that Scar and the Dirty Money Crew were a huge problem for the city of Baltimore, but she still fell victim to the allure of easy money. When she'd started taking his money, she didn't like Scar but could justify his actions and the reason to take the money, but now that he and his crew were influencing her family, she was growing to hate him and everything he stood for. She was ashamed that she'd never thought to do anything about the Dirty Money Crew, until they hit too close to home.

As she prepared to finally pull out of the restaurant's parking lot, she started thinking of ways to get Danielle away from the Dirty Money Crew's tight grip. As if a light bulb went off in her head, she thought of it. The perfect plan. She peeled out and began driving like a woman possessed.

Danielle had made it all the way home before calling Sticks. She and Veronica went over their lie a thousand times with a fine-tooth comb. They tried to think of every possible thing Sticks could ask. Danielle knew Sticks was just bold enough to call Veronica and interrogate her as well.

She dialed Sticks' number and nervously waited for him to pick up.

"Hey, baby," she said sweetly, desperately trying to hide her nerves. She lied and told him she was in the mall with Veronica when he had called her, that her phone didn't have a signal. From what Danielle could tell, it seemed as if Sticks had bought the story. He didn't ask as many questions as he normally did, which set her at ease. Sticks told her to be ready in two hours because he was coming to get her.

Danielle hung up from Sticks and rushed into her bathroom. She looked around to make sure her mother was busy counting the money from Maria. When she was sure her mother was good and distracted, she closed the door, ripped her pants down, and took a piss in a cup. Before she could even think about getting dressed to see Sticks, she had to have a question answered. She needed to be one hundred percent sure.

The last few days had been hard on Danielle. She

was throwing up the second she woke up, a sure sign of pregnancy. She tried to ignore it, but the feeling didn't seem to be going away. Danielle nervously stared down at the little white dipstick and waited, her heart beating like horse hoofs at the Kentucky Derby.

When the two lines showed up so quickly, she thought she was reading it wrong. She retrieved the box out of the garbage and read the back for the twentieth time. "Two pink lines mean pregnant," she said out loud. She grabbed the hair at both sides of her head and shook her head from side to side in disbelief. She and Sticks had been having unprotected sex, but he'd made her feel so damn good, she never worried about the consequences.

What the hell am I going to do now? she thought. Danielle put her back up against the bathroom door; slid down to the floor, and cried her eyes out. There was no way a baby would fit into her life right now. Besides, she didn't know what Sticks would think or say.

For the next two hours Danielle was walking around like a zombie, and before she knew it, Sticks was blowing up her phone again. She pulled herself together and went outside to meet him. Her mother's warnings as she left the house fell on deaf ears. Danielle was too distracted to even hear her. Her legs felt like they were made of melted butter as she walked to Sticks' car. She wasn't dressed like her usual sexy self, and by the look on his face, Sticks took immediate notice. She tried to smile to hide the fact that something was wrong, but her smile still appeared forced and fake.

"Hey, baby. I missed you," she sang as she slid into the passenger seat of the car.

Sticks was unmoved and unnervingly short with her. Danielle took notice too. Her mind started going crazy with wild thoughts. *Maybe he knows I'm pregnant,* she thought as butterflies danced in her stomach. She willed herself to stay calm.

"Yo, where you been?" Sticks asked out of the blue. He wanted to test her, to see if she would tell him a lie to his face. Loyalty was everything to him. He kept trying to give Danielle the benefit of the doubt. He really did love her, but being a snitch was unacceptable in his book, no matter who the person was. Even if it was his mama.

"I-I told you. I was at the mall with Veronica. You know how those fuckin' dead zones are up in that raggedy-ass mall. No signal." Danielle, unable to look Sticks in the eyes for fear she would burst out crying because of her secret, lowered her head and eyes. She knew it was his baby, but she was afraid he wouldn't take the news so well. She was scared he would accuse her of trying to trap him, and then he would leave her, or worse, beat her down like he had done twice before.

This bitch can't even look me in my eye. She is lying to my fuckin' face. I should murk her ass right here, Sticks thought to himself as he flexed his jaw. He hated when people lied to him, but what made this worse was, he truly loved this girl. He was seriously considering marrying her. Now he had no choice but to put an end to their relationship, and her life. Their relationship was now business, and no one fucked with his business. He had to think of something real good to take care of her ass.

"Yo, we moved the operation up to the day after tomorrow. You gonna be the front person," Sticks informed her.

"Me? I can't—I—I mean, I wouldn't be any good at that."

Danielle had only agreed to be a lookout or a driver for their upcoming operation. She had helped with the planning and logistics but wasn't ready to go to the front line. In fact, Sticks had told her she would be behind the scenes—a driver or a lookout—that she wouldn't ever have to get her hands dirty because he wouldn't want to put her in harm's way. But now he was changing up the game plan. Something didn't feel right to her. *Maybe it's just the pregnancy*, she thought.

Danielle's immediate hesitation and ultimate refusal was enough for Sticks. He was sure she was a snitch now. She'd always been down for whatever, since he had started fucking with her. That's why he loved her so much. Aside from the tight wetness she was walking around with between her legs. Sticks thought she was the most beautiful ride-or-die chick in all of Baltimore.

Sticks had watched her rob grown-ass hustlers in broad daylight. He had witnessed her beat down two female crackheads that owed him money, and he saw her exert authority over some of the real young crew members, keeping them in line like a mother hen. *Why the sudden change of heart?* he wondered. He quickly concluded that it was because she was working with either the feds or the local police and couldn't get her hands dirty.

Sticks had plans for Danielle. Knowing she was snitching had hurt him deep down inside. He didn't take lightly to anyone hurting his feelings, especially somebody he trusted so deeply. Good pussy or not, love or no love, in his eyes, Danielle was just like any other snitch and she would be handled as such.

They were both silent as Sticks drove toward the warehouse, each of them wondering what the other was thinking.

Danielle's hands were sweaty. She contemplated just telling him about the baby right then and there, but when she noticed his mood, she decided against it. She knew firsthand how violent Sticks could get when upset, so she opted to remain silent. *Maybe he will marry me and we can be a family,* she thought to herself.

Danielle promised herself to tell Sticks about their baby when he was in a better mood. Right now she would just try and ride out his mood.

Sticks looked over at the side of Danielle's beautiful face. *A fucking waste of beauty. Too bad. Shake it off, nigga,* he thought to himself. *She is a snitch.*

The nervous energy inside the Dirty Money Crew's warehouse was crazy. Some of them paced the floor, others drank liquor or lit up blunts, trying to calm their nerves.

"Yo, I'm ready to make this paper, dog," Timber

said, rubbing gun oil on the outside of his favorite gun, the AK-47 Sticks had given him.

"Calm down, nigga. We need to have this shit well thought out. I didn't think we were even fuckin' finished planning anyway." Trail didn't understand why Sticks was breaking out the gate with this shit when they were still in the planning phase.

Sticks, on edge for the past two days, barked, "Yo, you a bitch-ass nigga, and I'm sick of your fuckin' whining and complaining! Shut the fuck up and stop actin' like a straight bitch! The shit is as planned out as it's gonna get!"

"Fuck you, nigga! I'm tired of you tryin'a punk me in front of the young'uns," Trail shot back. It was like he had drunk a glass of liquid courage. He knew how crazy Sticks could get, but he was really fed up. For months he had watched as Sticks and the new members of the crew terrorized the city, bringing heat on all of them.

"What? What you say, nigga? I will body you right here and right now, word to everything. You punk bitch, you lucky Scar likes you," Sticks said, pointing his gun at Trail's head.

"Fuck this shit! Do this shit without me. We ain't ready yet." Trail stormed out of the warehouse. He had finally hit his breaking point. There was no way he was going to be a part of something as big as this without a well thought out plan of action.

"Go then, you scared-ass pussy!"

Sticks started having a bad gut feeling about going through with their plans too, but he couldn't let the young'uns see him sweat or think he was scared.

Deep down he knew Trail was right. There needed to be more planning, but with the thought of a snitch in his crew, and his hunger for power, he couldn't call it off. He mentally shook off his doubts and made his weapons ready for war.

"Fuck anybody who ain't down!" Sticks growled as he looked around into the faces of the young crew of gunners. All too afraid to reject his ideas, none of them dared to speak or express even a little bit of doubt. "A'ight then. Let's roll out," he yelled.

Danielle's heels clicked against the shiny marble floor of the bank. Dark shades covered her eyes as she stood behind a small counter and acted as if she was filling out a deposit or withdrawal slip. She carefully transcribed the note Sticks had provided to her word for word onto the bank's withdrawal slip. She looked around, trying not to show her nerves. She had a precise time to act. If she made one false move, everyone would be thrown off their role. She was the point person and everything going as planned depended on her.

She swallowed hard as Timber walked in, then Sticks, then two more of the crew. They fanned out and got into their rehearsed positions. Now all four corners of the bank were covered and being watched.

Danielle looked at her watch and exhaled. *Ten seconds left. Slide the paper under the glass. Tell the teller, "No funny business," and show her the gun. Slide the paper under the glass. Tell the teller, "No funny . . ."* She rehearsed her role over and over again in her head. She also thought about the alternate plan, just in case.

Danielle had been charged with shooting the little old security guard that stood by the customer service tables running his mouth, if something jumped off and he tried to break bad. Timber and the others would then take the counters and snatch as much money as they could get.

Sticks was there just to ensure everything went according to the time frame. He usually had these things mapped out. Eight minutes was all they had from the time they walked in until the time they reached their getaway car.

Danielle swallowed hard. She felt sweat dripping down the sides of her face as her stomach did somersaults. The time had finally arrived. She walked slowly to the middle teller, as she was instructed. See, Sticks had found out from an insider at the bank that the middle teller didn't have the panic button in front of her station. She would either have to lean left or right, which would tell them if she was trying to push it.

"Good morning, ma'am. How can I help you today?" the teller asked, not really paying too much attention to the customer standing in front of her.

Danielle silently pushed the slip of paper under the small opening in the glass. The teller's eyes popped open and she looked around nervously as soon as she read the words. Now she was paying attention to the customer standing in front of her.

The teller immediately looked left and locked eyes with Timber, who smiled at her and patted his waistband to let her know not to try anything funny. Then the teller started to notice the other members of the crew sprinkled around, sticking out like sore thumbs amongst the regular bank customers.

"Ma'am, how would you like your bills counted out?" she asked, trying to remain calm.

"I don't have a preference," Danielle coolly replied.

"I have to get some more tens," the teller said. "I will be right back."

Danielle figured the teller was probably getting a bag to put the stacks of money in because she had been warned in the note about panic buttons, dye packs, and calling the cops.

Sticks watched the teller from a distance. He noticed her give the teller to her right a little side glance. Then the other teller looked down and reached for something. Sticks tapped his foot impatiently. He figured whatever the middle teller had said to Danielle was a code for the other teller to push her panic button.

That was enough for Sticks. He walked over to Danielle, who looked up at him as if to say, *What the fuck are you doing? Are you crazy?*

"Honey, we gotta go. We can stop at another bank on the way out of town," he said, grabbing onto Danielle's arm.

"On the way out of town" was the signal to abort the robbery. Danielle quickly followed Sticks' lead and split.

When Timber noticed them rushing to try to get out of the bank, he lost it. "What the fuck is you doin', nigga?! I ain't leavin' outta here without some paper!" he screamed loudly, pulling his gun from his pants.

Screams erupted all over the bank. People began running for the doors, and some got down on the floor.

Meanwhile, the little old security guard tried to draw his weapon, but before he could even hoist it up, one of the younger crew members shot him dead. *Bang! Bang! Bang!* "Yo! Let's go, nigga!!" Sticks screamed to Timber.

Danielle began running for the door, but the other security guard tried to grab her. Timber lit him up with his semi-automatic, and the guard's blood sprayed on her face and clothes, making her sick and weak. The adrenaline pumping through her body and the baby in her belly was a bad combination. Danielle felt like she would faint at any minute.

Timber continued to spray at random. The inside of the bank was pure pandemonium now, with bodies dropping from his reckless bullets. He jumped up on the counter, but the bulletproof glass was too high for him to climb over it. When the tellers had all fled to the bank's emergency robbery shelter, Timber got so angry, he started shooting more of the bank's patrons at random.

Sticks heard the distant wail of sirens. He was finally out the door. Whoever wasn't with him would just be left behind.

Danielle was right behind him but starting to fall farther behind. Trying to keep up with him, she kicked off her heels and tried running barefoot, but she was too weak to pick up speed.

Sticks knew they had a car waiting for them one block up, but they hadn't given the driver the signal to come get them from the front of the bank. He took off down the street, but the block was beginning to fill up with cops.

Timber was now hot on Sticks' heels, but Danielle had fallen farther back, her chest burning with each step.

"Police! Drop your weapons!" a cop screamed at them.

Timber turned and opened fire, hitting the officer right in the head.

"Get the fuck in, nigga!" Sticks screamed to Timber as he and Timber got to the getaway car.

Danielle was still coming toward them, trying hard to make it. Winded, she continued struggling, running for her life. She heard loud pops as the cops opened fire on them, and bullets whizzed by her head.

Sticks jumped into the truck, and so did Timber.

"Wait!" Danielle screamed, tears and makeup streaking her face. It looked like they were leaving her.

"Put it in reverse! Reverse out the block!" Sticks screamed.

The driver did as he was told.

Danielle was almost there, but then they started moving away from her. "What are y'all doin'?" she screamed. "Sticks!" The faster she ran, the farther away the getaway truck went.

"Do it now, nigga!" Sticks yelled.

Timber extended his arm out of the window and opened fire on Danielle. The police were also shooting at her.

Danielle felt hot metal searing through her skin.

Her eyes bulged in shock and pain. She was in disbelief that her own crew had set her up. As her legs stopped moving, she thought about the baby she was carrying and the great betrayal she had just suffered. Then she gave up. Her bullet-ridden body lurched forward and hit the ground with a splat. She felt the life leaving her. "Why, Sticks, why?" She gurgled as blood spilled from her mouth.

Within no time her limp, lifeless body was surrounded by the police.

Sticks, Timber, and the driver jumped out of the truck they were in and changed to a smaller car they had stashed a few miles away, just in case something like this had jumped off. Sticks knew at least three members of their crew were dead and the rest of the young'uns were going to be hemmed up by the cops. He couldn't look back now. He knew he wouldn't have trouble recruiting replacements into the Dirty Money Crew. But the thought of replacing Danielle gave him instant heartburn.

"Damn, man, I thought Dani was your main bitch," the driver said.

"That bitch was a snitch," Timber replied before Sticks could say anything. "We was gonna kill her ass after this anyway. We just wanted her to help us get this last big lick before we murked her informant ass."

Sticks didn't really have the heart to stand in front of her and just kill her, so he had instructed Timber to make sure her death looked like it was a result of the bank robbery. He still had too much love for her. In his own world, thinking about Danielle, Sticks remained silent as they rode in the opposite direction of the racing police cars. He was hurting inside.

"Who the fuck is banging on my door this time of night?" Dana grumbled as she rushed to her front door. "Better not be this Danielle talking about she forgot her damn keys. Who is it?" Dana called out.

"Baltimore County Police!" a booming baritone on the other side of the door replied.

Dana screwed up her face and yanked the door open. She thought maybe Danielle had been picked up for something.

"Ms. Rodriguez?" the officer asked.

"No. My last name is Thomas. My daughter's last name is Rodriguez," Dana said nervously. A sick feeling washed over her.

"Can we come in, ma'am?" one of the officers asked.

Dana moved aside, and the officers stepped into her home.

"Ma'am, we are sorry to tell you that your daughter Danielle Rodriguez has been killed."

Dana's ears started ringing, and she couldn't move. A scream was welling up inside of her, ready to erupt. She opened her mouth, and the sound that escaped was almost like that of a pig at slaughter. She fell to her knees and screamed, "Nooooo!" at the top of her lungs.

The officers tried to help her up, but Dana would not move from that spot. She was wracked with sobs, and her body trembled.

After a few minutes on her knees wailing uncontrollably, she allowed the officers to help her up.

"What happened?" she yelled. "Why my child?"

"Ma'am, your daughter was killed fleeing the scene of a bank robbery. She was with a group of men that tried to rob the bank," one of the officers informed Dana.

"You must be mistaken! My daughter wouldn't do something like that! She is a good girl! Danielle knows better! I don't believe you!" Dana belted out, flailing her arms at the officers.

"Ms. Thomas, I'm afraid it was your daughter." The officer shoved a picture of Danielle's bloodied body toward Dana.

Dana placed her hand over her mouth. It was Danielle in the picture. "Would you please call her sister? She is a cop too," she managed to say.

The officers looked shocked, like they thought she was lying.

"Her card ... it's on the counter. Please call. I can't . . . I just can't," she said, breaking down with tears all over again.

Maria Rodriguez was in her bed when her cell phone began vibrating. She looked at the screen and saw a strange phone number. "Hello?" she answered cautiously.

"Yes, this is Officer Rodriguez," she replied to the strange caller. Rodriguez sat up in the bed. "About my sister? What about her? Has something happened?" she asked, a pang of nervousness punching through her gut.

After the caller instructed her to come down to the hospital, she jumped out of the bed and began throwing on any piece of clothing she could find. She instinctively grabbed her gun and badge and busted out the front door. She raced her car through the streets of Baltimore, running all red lights on the way as her heart beat out of her chest. *Please let this girl be okay,* she thought.

When she arrived at the county hospital, she flew down the hallways, almost knocking people down several times. She finally noticed a gathering of cops and rushed over to where they stood.

"Hi, I'm Officer Rodriguez. Someone called me about my sister?" she said, trying to catch her breath.

Rodriguez didn't recognize any of the Baltimore County officers there. As a state trooper, she sometimes worked with the local county cops, but not often enough to know them on a first-name basis or by sight.

"Officer Rodriguez, I am Lieutenant Brady, Baltimore County." A tall, white-haired man extended his hand for a shake.

"What is going on with my Danielle?" Rodriguez asked, ignoring the lieutenant's hand. She was feeling worse about this whole scene by the second.

"I'm sorry, Officer Rodriguez," the lieutenant said in a low tone, trying to soften the blow. "Your sister is gone."

Rodriguez thought she hadn't heard correctly, so she asked the lieutenant to repeat himself. When he did, she hollered, "No!"

Rodriguez began banging the wall next to her so

hard, her hand felt as if it would break. Even with the pain, she couldn't stop punching. She wanted to rip somebody's head off. She had warned Danielle, had told her about that crew. She had promised herself since she was a child that she wouldn't shed tears. This was different, uncontrollable. She couldn't keep them from falling.

"How did this happen?" she croaked out, tears burning at the back of her eyes.

"Our initial reports say she was shot by her own people while they ran from the scene of an attempted bank robbery," the lieutenant explained.

Rodriguez immediately knew who was responsible. She could only wonder if they'd found out Danielle was her sister and took it out on her.

"I want the autopsy, toxicology, and DNA reports back as soon as possible," Rodriguez told the lieutenant. "I want to be involved and informed about all the developments in this case. I am her sister."

The lieutenant didn't argue.

Rodriguez knew right away who she would make pay for Danielle's death. The Dirty Money Crew had taken away her only sibling. She stormed out of the building. She needed time to think and regroup.

Once outside, she immediately began plotting the downfall of the entire Dirty Money Crew, including Scar Johnson.

Rodriguez and Dana sat in the front row together at the funeral, hand in hand, hoping they could make it through such a tragic day. As Rodriguez stared at

Danielle's stiff corpse, she found new fervor to take Scar down.

Rodriguez hadn't slept in a week since finding out about Danielle's death. Wracked with guilt, she could hardly stand to look at herself in a mirror. She had always thought of herself as a stand-up cop, but now she doubted herself as a cop, a sister, a daughter, and as a person in general. She realized she hadn't been strong enough to stand up to Scar and say no when he'd approached her the first time. Blinded by the money, and fearing for her own safety, she took part in Scar's web of murder, lies, and deceit. Well, things had changed. She wasn't afraid anymore. She was pissed, and didn't care if Scar exposed her and the deal they had cut. She didn't care if she lost her job. She just wanted to avenge her dear sister's death by getting Scar and his little murderous crew off the streets.

What devastated her most was when the medical examiner told her that Danielle was pregnant. Not only did Rodriguez lose her sister, but she also lost her chance to be an auntie. She didn't even bother to tell their mother about that because her mother wanted to be a grandmother more than anything and wouldn't have been able to handle it.

Rodriguez needed some sort of redemption. Suddenly, it was now her mission in life to help get young kids off the streets and to show that life under Scar's direction wasn't the American dream but really a nightmare.

Chapter 6

Closure

Derek stared at Tiphani in shock and awe. He was so surprised she had come to visit him, he could hardly keep his mouth closed. She looked extra beautiful to him now. Derek missed seeing her beautiful face with its exotic features. He still thought she was the most beautiful woman in the world. Her perfume filled his nostrils and made his dick hard.

Derek sat frozen, holding out hope that his wife had come to tell him she wanted him back. He didn't even care whether or not she ever apologized; he just wanted his life back. And he knew Tiphani was talented enough a lawyer to help him get out of jail.

"Well, I know this is awkward," Tiphani started. She could barely hold eye contact with Derek, who looked horrible in the orange prison jumpsuit. His skin was ashy and drawn up, and he looked like he had lost fifty pounds. His full beard swallowed up his face, and she could see the signs of stress in his red, hopeless eyes. She did notice that his eyes lit up when he saw her, which didn't flatter her at all, but made her feel sorry for him for a brief moment.

"Thanks for coming to see me. I don't get many visitors, unless my attorney decides to come," Derek said, half-jokingly, trying to lighten the tension between them.

There was an awkward silence. The air in the room felt much the same way the courtroom did the day Derek was convicted, thick and almost suffocating.

"How are my little ones? Are you all right? Do you know who did the kidnapping? Did they hurt you at all?" Derek rattled off, trying to fill the awkward silence.

Tiphani ignored every one of his questions. "I came for a specific reason. This," she said, sliding a set of newly drawn up divorce papers across the table toward him. She didn't have time for small talk, nor did she want to have any with her soon-to-be ex-husband. She wanted to get to the point and get out.

Derek was in shock when he looked down at the papers. Seeing them took his breath away and he stopped breathing for what felt like a few minutes. They'd had their fair share of ups and downs and even an ugly, drawn-out custody battle when he was a free man. But somewhere in the back of his mind, he'd always thought they might work things out.

He lifted his shackled hands and picked up the papers to examine them more closely. DIVORCE DECREE, it read. Derek felt like his heart split in two. If being in prison hadn't broken him, this did.

"Tiphani, I'm sorry. I don't know what else to say. I still love you. I need you. You and the kids are all I've got. Can we please work things out? " Derek gripped the papers in his hand so tightly, he was inadvertently crumpling them.

"Look, let's just get this all over with," Tiphani replied, a smirk on her face. The more Derek begged, the weaker he looked to her, which turned her off all over again. Tiphani wasn't stupid. She knew her husband's manipulative ways well. She knew he just wanted somebody to stick by him and help him try to appeal his conviction.

Tiphani was still bitter. She couldn't forget the way Derek had treated her after the incident with Scar, calling her all types of whores in front of her colleagues in family court. She wasn't going to forgive him. They were done.

"Tiphani, why don't you think this over and reconsider? Think about the kids." Derek felt tears welling up, but he refused to let her see him cry. He felt like he had been stripped of his dignity in enough ways already.

"Look, Derek, what don't you understand? We are done. Over. I don't want you anymore. I have moved on, so you should do the same. I am over you and all of this. I am just here to make it official and legal. Now sign the papers and do us both a favor."

Derek hung his head in defeat. He could tell by her callous attitude that his wife had been corrupted by his brother. He knew it was a strong possibility that she and Scar were still together, maybe living like one big happy family with his kids, now that she was home safe. The thought of Tiphani and Scar together made Derek's insides boil. He still found it hard to believe that the woman that once loved him so much could now hate him so deeply.

Biting down into his jaw, he picked up the pen and began signing the divorce papers. As he wrote his name on the line, he thought more and more about his brother's betrayal. About Tiphani's betrayal too.

"This is what you and Scar had planned all along, isn't it? To destroy me over lust? Is dick that important to you? You know good and damn well where Scar is. You probably faked the whole fuckin' kidnapping too, you cold-hearted bitch!"

Derek's sadness had now turned to unbridled anger that he needed to let loose. If he wasn't shackled, he felt like he probably would've punched Tiphani until her face caved in. Because of the commotion he was causing, the COs began moving toward the table as his voice rose higher and higher.

"I hate you, bitch!" he screamed. "You know what goes around comes around! You and Scar will get yours! You think he is gonna love you like I did? He won't! You hear me? He won't! He is using you just like he used me! I'm his flesh and blood, and he betrayed me, so imagine you! You're just a piece of pussy to him! You are replaceable in Scar's world! You better think about what you're doing! Don't be stupid!"

The COs grabbed his arms and began dragging him out of the room.

Tiphani remained composed. She heard what Derek was saying but gave it no thought or credence. Scar loved her, and she knew it. Derek was just jealous.

She gathered up the signed divorce papers and watched as her husband made a total ass of himself. She felt relieved when she looked down at his signature. Cutting off all ties with him was what she needed to succeed.

Tiphani felt good inside. She finally had closure.

Chapter 7

Out of the Shadows

The Shadow was lying in bed thinking about the news that the Dirty Money Crew had lost a few bodies in a botched bank heist. Now was the perfect time to get on the inside. They were short of men and were going to need to fill the ranks. But how? was the question. You couldn't exactly just walk up to the front door and say, "I want to join."

Many different scenarios were playing out in the Shadow's mind, but none seemed right. The Shadow had done such a good job of keeping a safe distance from Scar and his crew that there was no contact with any of them.

Taking down Scar's crew was an obsession that was turning maniacal. It was all the Shadow thought about, and now the time had come to take it to the next level and destroy Scar and the Dirty Money Crew. There was no more surveillance to be done, no more information to be gathered. Everything that could be known from the outside was known. Now, the information obtained had to be put to use on the inside.

Throughout his surveillance, the Shadow kept following Scar and his crew to a specific check cashing place. He thought the Dirty Money Crew was looking to take the place down. Some of the younger bucks tried forcing their way in through the front door but were quickly met with some retaliatory force and had to run because the cops had been called. After that incident, the Crew backed off the place, which seemed to be the Fort Knox of check cashing places. No one was going to get in. The Shadow figured robbing this place would be the way into the Dirty Money Crew.

It had been three weeks of watching this place all day, every day, from the front of the store to the back. They ran a tight ship, and robbing it seemed damn near impossible. The more the Shadow watched, the tighter the security seemed to appear. In fact, the Shadow saw no weakness. Almost all hope was lost, and the Shadow had decided he was just going to try and blast through the front door.

But then the Shadow observed something. While staking out the back alley, he saw the woman who worked at the check cashing walk out the back door of the nail salon two stores down. It had never occurred to him, but the workers at the check cashing place never left the building all day. There was no back door, and none of them ever left through the front, not even to get lunch.

When he saw the worker leave through the back door of the nail salon, it finally made sense. Somehow the nail salon and the check cashing place were connected. That's how they were getting in and out during the day. He just had to figure out how they were connected. That was the way in to the check cashing and the Dirty Money Crew. The Shadow was hyped and couldn't wait to take this place down.

Immediately the Shadow thought it was a good day to get a manicure. His nails were looking a little raggedy. After bullshitting with the ladies at the nail salon and gaining their trust, he went to the bathroom, which was conveniently located in the back of the salon. There wasn't much time to snoop around. A person could be in the bathroom for only so long before people started checking on them.

The Shadow started opening every door that was visible. Nothing but supply closets and tanning booths. He stood in front of the back door and tried to figure out how the two stores were connected. That's when the Shadow saw it. It wasn't easy to spot, but there was a door that looked exactly like the wall. No doorknob, just a little hole so a person could grab it and slide it. It was a pocket door that slid sideways into the wall.

Sensing he didn't have much time, the Shadow quickly opened it. He saw a downward set of stairs. He ran down the stairs and saw that they led to a long tunnel that ran underneath the store next to the salon. *I bet this leads right to the check cashing place*, he thought. Back up the stairs and into the bathroom he went.

Almost instantly one of the salon workers came knocking on the bathroom door to make sure everything was okay.

"Just have an upset stomach," he said. "I'm finishing up in here." The Shadow came out of the bathroom, said good-bye, and walked out of the salon. He was now one step closer to taking down the Dirty Money Crew.

Dressed in all black with a wool-knit face mask, the Shadow easily broke into the salon in the middle of the night and was now hiding in the tunnel, where he was going to wait until morning. The plan was to ambush the first person to come through the tunnel. Since it would be first thing in the morning, whoever came through the tunnel was definitely going to be surprised. Another advantage to doing the stickup first thing was, there wouldn't be as many people working, or waiting to cash checks. The Shadow was hoping to get in and out.

After waiting several hours, the Shadow couldn't stay awake. The long hours of following Scar, Sticks, and anyone involved with Dirty Money Crew nonstop were taking a toll. It was a much-needed rest.

Deep in sleep and dreaming of the good life, the Shadow was startled awake by the sliding open of the door to the tunnel. Immediately the hand went to the gun. He was ready to pounce.

Crouching down in the darkest part of the tunnel, he waited as the unsuspecting victim walked right into the trap. When they were in range, the Shadow jumped up and pointed the gun in the face of the middle-aged woman who worked at the check cashing place, catching her completely off guard.

"Hands up, bitch!" the Shadow growled. "You wit' anyone?"

The woman lost control of her bowels and shit herself right there on the spot. Speechless, she just stood there with her hands up, eyes bulging, staring at him.

"Speak!" he demanded.

"I—I—I'm alone," she stuttered. "I come early to open up from the inside. Please don't hurt me," she said through heaving sobs. "Please."

"Do what I tell you, and no one will get hurt. Start walking."

They made their way through the tunnel and up into the back room of the check cashing place, the woman crying and pleading for her life the whole time. The smell of shit was getting awful. Once inside, the Shadow directed the woman to open the safe.

"I can't. I only know the combination to the mini safe."

"Who can open the main safe?"

"Big Mike. But he won't be in for at least thirty minutes."

The Shadow had a decision to make. Wait for Big Mike, or just take what was available right now and hope it was enough to impress Sticks. "What's in the mini safe?"

"Not much. Just the cash we use for the drawer."

"Open it!" The Shadow stuck the gun in her face for maximum effect.

The woman was so nervous, her hands were trembling, and she kept messing up the combination.

"Hurry the fuck up!" The Shadow hit the woman

upside her head with the butt end of the gun, opening a gash in her head.

Blood soaking her hair and pouring down her neck, the woman yelped like a dog and started back to the lock. This time she was able to open the safe.

As soon as it was open, the Shadow reached in and took the contents out. There was three thousand dollars in cash and about forty thousand dollars in calling cards, which made the Shadow more than happy. He placed the calling cards and cash in a duffel bag. Then before leaving, he hog-tied the woman with electrical tape.

Being careful to avoid being seen by anyone coming into the nail salon, the Shadow snuck out the back door and walked to the waiting getaway car a block away.

Word about the robbery spread through the streets like wild fire. The Dirty Money Crew was trying desperately to find out who did it, but no one knew.

Sticks was starting to become paranoid. He thought one of his guys did it and wasn't telling him. If word got out that one of his guys was doing something behind his back, it would signal to the streets that he didn't have control, and the streets would lose respect for him, meaning, he would now have a bull's-eye on his back. He felt like his very life depended on finding out who robbed the check cashing place.

***

Timber was standing guard outside of the warehouse, passing the time by working on his rhymes.
He had dreams of becoming a rapper and thought
he could someday use his connections in the crime
world to get him a record deal. He figured, a lot of
other rappers had started out slingin' rocks and then
went on to stardom, so why couldn't he do it?

As he spat his lyrics, a figure walked up to the gate
of the warehouse. Timber stopped rapping. "Got a
problem, mu'fucka?" He stared directly into the person's eyes, letting them know he wasn't afraid.

"I wanna come in."

"Who the fuck is you?" Timber put his hand on the
pistol in his waistband.

"I robbed the check cashing spot."

Timber wasn't expecting to hear that. "Who says?"

Staying calm, the Shadow opened up the duffel
bag and showed Timber the calling cards. "I want to
fence these."

Seeing the calling cards made Timber a believer.
Not taking his eyes off the Shadow, he yelled out,
"Ay, yo," which was the code for the other workers to
open the gate to the warehouse.

The warehouse, as usual, had about twenty guys in
it, all smoking blunts. Some were counting money,
others were bagging dope.

This was the first time the Shadow had ever been
inside. He was taking mental notes, just in case this
was the last time as well.

"Yo!" Timber barked at the top of his lungs, "this
the nigga that took down the check cashing spot."

Everyone in the warehouse instantly stopped what

they were doing and turned to look at the person who did what none of them was able to do. All talking and movement stopped. The warehouse got so quiet, it was as if no one was even breathing.

Timber and the Shadow stood in the middle of the warehouse in full view of everyone, like animals in a zoo. The Shadow was just taking it all in, the exits, how many dudes were there, how many guns, everything. If this was gonna be his only time in the warehouse, he wanted to be sure to remember every last detail.

The silence was broken by footsteps at the back of the warehouse. It was Sticks coming from the back office. He slowly walked across the warehouse. The tension in the warehouse was thick. All of the crew just watched and waited to see what he would do.

Sticks knew that everyone was watching him, which made him walk slower. He was trying to show this new jack who was boss, that he didn't have to hurry for no one. "This nigga here?" Sticks said, a condescending smirk on his face.

The tension in the air dissipated as everyone in the warehouse laughed. With that one little remark, Sticks let everyone know that he wasn't afraid of this new jack, that he had the situation under control. All of the young bucks in the crew were reassured that they had put their trust in the right man, that no one would be gunning for Sticks anytime soon.

"So you the man that took down the check cash spot?" Sticks eyed the Shadow with caution.

"That's right, and I want to fence these calling cards." The Shadow came back cool as ice. "You interested?"

"Come back to the office where we can discuss business in private," Sticks countered.

The two men were playing a game with each other, both striving to gain the upper hand, neither man wanting to show weakness. They made their way through the warehouse and into the office, where Sticks sat at his desk and directed the new jack to sit across from him.

"First off, who the fuck are you? I ain't never seen you before."

"Day. My name is Day."

"Day. A'ight. Where you from, Day?" Sticks wasn't ready to trust this dude yet. He was thinking, *Some guy just shows up out of the blue, robs a spot, and no one knows who he is. That's not exactly someone you just welcome with open arms.*

"I'm from Pittsburgh. Hill District. Was born here, so I decided to come back. Needed a change of scenery. You know how it is, kind of wore out my welcome. Five-O may be on the lookout for me up there."

"I hear you. You know, we been wantin' to take that spot for a minute," Sticks said, starting to feel more at ease with this dude.

"No, I didn't know. Great minds think alike," Day joked.

Sticks smiled then got serious. "How you do something alone that my whole crew couldn't do together?"

"Careful planning and execution." Day didn't want to give up too much information. He figured, the less he had to say, the better.

"Why that spot? And why come to us?" Sticks was

being very cautious with Day. He was intrigued by this guy but still on guard.

"The spot was random. Everyone knows you the only game in town. You want to do business or not? I'm not a cop, so there's no need for all these questions. If you don't want these calling cards, someone else will. I just came to you because you the most professional niggas in B-more. I figured it'd be easier dealing with you than some of these wild-ass niggas out there." Day opened his bag to show Sticks the calling cards and move the proceedings along. He didn't like all the questions and was hoping that his bluff about taking business elsewhere would work.

But Sticks liked getting his ego stroked. Being told he was the only game in town and the most professional made him feel like a king and took him off his guard a bit. When Day opened his bag, Sticks saw the calling cards and did some quick math in his head. The cards could easily be sold on the streets for a nice little profit.

Sticks, thinking about what to do, sat back and stared at Day. He knew he was going to take the cards, but was he going to actually buy them or take them by force? On the one hand, no one knew this dude, so no one would miss him, but on the other hand, Sticks kind of liked this cat. He was obviously smart, and he definitely had some balls, robbing a spot that none of his crew could. And Sticks admired that.

"A'ight, I'll take the cards—"

"For how much?" Day said, cutting Sticks off before he could finish his sentence.

"Whoa! Hold on, young buck. Relax. I'll take the

cards, but let's talk real business first." Sticks leaned forward in his chair. "You need to join the Dirty Money Crew."

Day sat there in shock, but stayed stone-faced throughout. This was exactly what he wanted and was much easier than he thought it would be. In fact, he couldn't believe it was actually happening. *I need to play this right,* he thought. "I don't know. I'm kind of a lone wolf. I do my best work alone," he said, trying not to sound too eager.

"Word. I hear that, but why be a lone wolf, when you could have the protection of the whole pack?"

Day nodded his head like he was really giving it some thought.

"Look at it this way. You could have the whole pack with you or against you. Do you want to be the hunter or the hunted?"

Just what Day wanted to hear, a threat from Sticks. He already knew he was going to hook up with the crew, but he needed Sticks to feel superior and in charge. He wanted Sticks to feel as comfortable as possible around him, and thought one way was to let him feel smarter and tougher.

"You make a persuasive argument. I'm no match against you and your men. Seems to me the only smart decision here is to say yes."

Sticks smiled. He wanted to keep this dude close. He envisioned big things for the two of them together. Every boss needed a right-hand man, and Sticks thought he might have just found his. "I like your thinking. Now, let's smoke a blunt to celebrate," he said, pulling out a bag of weed and dropping it on the desk.

Day smiled at Sticks. "I think that's a good idea."

As Day sat there calmly watching Sticks roll a blunt, all he could think was, *This is the beginning of the end for you, you dumb mu'fucka!*

Chapter 8

Politics as Usual

Mayor Mathias Steele stood at the podium, signaling the beginning of the press conference. It was time to announce the Baltimore County judgeships. He was confident in the appointments that had been made. The media had cameras started rolling, and he was ready to proceed. "It is my honor to present the newly appointed justice of the Baltimore County circuit court, Ms. Tiphani Fuller." The mayor flashed his winning smile.

Flashbulbs sparkled in the crowd as Tiphani took her place next to the mayor on the stage. Dressed conservatively in a navy blue Anne Klein suit, she already resembled a government official. Smiling from ear to ear, she put her hand up and waved to the crowd. She was amazed at how smoothly things had been going for her.

"First, I'd like to thank God and my children for

giving me the will to live and to fight through my ordeal. Fighting my captors off wasn't easy, just as I
know helping the city of Baltimore fight crime will
not be easy either. I am honored to be appointed as
your circuit court judge. I plan to serve you with in-
tegrity and dignity. Surviving a violent kidnapping
has made me a stronger person. I promise you, I will
enlist justice to a system that has been broken and
marred with corruption. I just thank you again for
trusting me," she said, smiling and waving again like
a newly crowned beauty pageant contestant.

More bulbs flashed as Tiphani and Mayor Steele
posed for the perfect photo op. He pulled Tiphani close to him, a fake smile plastered on his face.
Tiphani and Mayor Steele had history, and in order
to keep what they shared in the past, he'd agreed to
grant her whatever she needed.

Mayor Steele was expected to win the state senate
seat, but he knew one wrong move or one bit of dirty
information being leaked could cost him. He was just
hoping that his support for Tiphani didn't backfire
on him.

Tiphani was also in full support of Mayor Steele's
bid for the senate seat. She knew that if he won she
would definitely be able to help Scar become the biggest, most connected player in the game.

Tiphani had four gowns laid out on her bed for
her victory celebration. She planned to be the center of attention at the party being held in her honor.
Sometimes she still couldn't believe how her life was

going. It seemed that everything just fell into place for her, and she was the first to admit, she deserved every bit of what she got. She picked up a lavender-colored Badgley Mischka from the bed and held it up to herself. She twirled around in the mirror like a little girl who had just gotten a new dress for Easter. She would be stunning, and she knew it.

Tiphani's personal hair stylist put her jet-black hair up into a neat bun, and her makeup artist gave her a very natural look, which accentuated her high cheek-bones. The pair of professionals had made Tiphani look and feel like a million bucks.

After her assistants were done making her up, she slid into her dress and examined herself carefully. She hadn't felt this good about herself in a long time. Staring at herself in the mirror, she thought she looked gorgeous. She kissed her kids good night and headed out to the party.

When Tiphani arrived at the city's largest catering hall, she made a grand entrance. There were hundreds of people in attendance—politicians; high-profile attorneys; several of her former colleagues from the DA's office, and a small group of police officers and state troopers. Everyone was there to support her, but more importantly to make sure they got face time with her. The private attorneys and prosecutors wanted to make sure she liked them, so things would go their way in the courtroom; the cops wanted to make face with her, so she'd always sign their search warrants, even in the middle of the night; and the politicians needed to keep Tiphani as an ace in their pockets, not knowing when their dirty dealings would be exposed.

Tiphani smiled and waved and made her way through the crowd. She felt better than she had on her own wedding day. As she worked the crowd, saying hello and accepting congratulations, she noticed Rodriguez, who was standing alone watching her. *What the fuck is she doing here?* she thought to herself, but she kept her plastic smile plastered on her face as she dodged bodies, making her way across the room.

Tiphani always had the feeling that Rodriguez never really cared for her. At first she thought it was because of Rodriguez's loyalty to Derek, but when Rodriguez had gotten down with her and Scar to set Derek up, she knew that wasn't the case. She just couldn't figure out what it was about Rodriguez that gave her the creeps.

One thing was for sure. Tiphani wasn't worried about Rodriguez revealing anything about her and Scar right now. She and Rodriguez both had secrets about each other that could easily destroy one another. The difference now was that Tiphani was not aware that since Danielle's death, Rodriguez was at the point that she did not care if her corrupt behavior was made public. Rodriguez was ready to face the consequence of her actions. She just wasn't ready to tell on herself.

Tiphani was smiling and speaking to some of the other judges when she noticed Rodriguez making her way toward her. She kept the fake smile plastered to her face. "Excuse me," she said to the group of people she had been speaking to, her face becoming serious.

"Tiphani, how are you? Congratulations. You look

great," Rodriguez said, grabbing her into a rough, awkward hug.

"Rodriguez, I'm surprised to see you here." Tiphani giggled.

Rodriguez let her out of the hug and looked into her face. Her expression was serious. She moved her face closer to Tiphani's. "I hope you're finished with your little affair with Scar Johnson, now that you are a big-time circuit court judge," she whispered, leaning into Tiphani's ear.

Tiphani's body stiffened, and she pursed her lips. The air swirling around them was thick with tension. "I am glad to see you, Rodriguez. Thank you for coming out to support me. Please don't hesitate to let me know if you ever need anything," she said, straightening out her gown. She started to turn around as several more of her supporters approached her.

"Funny you should ask. I will be contacting you real soon about a person we both have in common," Rodriguez called out loudly, garnering stares from others in the crowd. "Do I need to make an appointment, Judge Fuller?"

"Just get in touch with my clerk," Tiphani replied, rushing away.

Tiphani spent the rest of the night showing good face with her supporters. She even danced a few times.

Although Tiphani seemed fine, Rodriguez' visit and words were gnawing at the back of her mind. She left the hall and climbed into a waiting black Lincoln Town Car. She eased into the backseat, pulled off her shoes, and leaned her head back. The driver already knew where to take her.

I could get used to this, she thought to herself. *I just wish Scar was here to celebrate our work.* Her cell phone began buzzing inside her clutch. She hadn't looked at her phone all night long. She lifted her head off the backseat and retrieved her phone from the slim bag.

"Hello," she answered in a sultry voice, a mixture of happiness and exhaustion. "Hello?"

Still there was no answer on the other end. She looked at the screen, and the call disconnected.

She placed the phone up against her chest and smiled. She knew immediately it was Scar calling to let her know that phase two of the plan was about to go into effect. Scar was about to reappear, and before she knew it, he would be sitting in front of her in her new courtroom.

Tiphani felt like she owed Scar everything. Not only did she feel a great sense of loyalty to him, she loved him. She vowed to do everything in her new judicial power to help Scar clear himself of the charges against him.

Scar hung up his cell phone and turned his attention back to the beautiful woman lying in his bed. He walked over and gave her a deep kiss. She returned his kiss and opened her legs to allow him into her. Scar thought about Tiphani briefly. He knew he didn't love her or want to be with her, but he was hoping that she believed that he did.

As Scar moved his dick in and out of his newest beauty, he only hoped that he had Tiphani wrapped around his finger as much as he thought he did.

Chapter 9

I'm Back

Sticks and Trail embraced Scar with a hug, pat, and pound. "Damn, nigga! You look relaxed," Sticks commented, giving Scar the once-over. Trail was smiling at Scar just for good measure, but he was seriously biting his tongue. He was waiting to get Scar alone, to fill him in on his boy Sticks' power trip.

"Lots of good sun, good food, and good pussy will do that to a nigga," Scar said, laughing at his own joke.

"I'm glad you back, my dude. Shit has been different without you," Trail said, casting sidelong glances in Sticks' direction.

Scar climbed into his Escalade and allowed Sticks to drive. As they rode down the highway, Sticks blabbed on and on about how the Dirty Money Crew was on the serious come-up under his direction, painting a picture of himself like he was the hardest gangster since Pablo Escobar. Trail just listened and laughed to himself, feeling like Sticks would eventually get his.

Scar, listening to Sticks' grand stories, suddenly spotted a trooper's car hiding in the bushes. He quickly reached over and grabbed the steering wheel, causing Sticks to swerve.

"Oh, shit! Nigga, what you doin'?" Sticks screamed out.

Scar knew exactly what he was doing.

The next thing they knew, blue and white lights were flashing behind them, just as Scar expected. He was extra calm and collected, mentally prepared for what was next. He had purposely not alerted his little henchmen to his plans, thinking they would try and stop him, and he didn't feel like dealing with their bullshit.

"Awww, fuck! What's up with this shit, Scar?" Sticks asked, his entire body shaking.

Trail was calm. He knew Scar must've known what he was doing.

"Give me y'all burners. Hurry the fuck up!" Scar instructed.

Sticks and Trail quickly took their guns and handed them to Scar, who put one gun in his waistband and one in the back of his pants.

The state trooper finally approached the car and knocked on the window. Sticks slowly rolled the window down. Before the trooper could ask for the registration, he noticed Scar in the passenger seat and fled back to his patrol car, where he went over the radio and called for backup. He didn't even have to say why he needed backup once he said he had Scar Johnson pulled over. Scar was back!

In less than five minutes his truck was surrounded by state troopers with their guns drawn and ready. Scar was called out of the car with at least fifteen guns trained on him. Before his feet could fully touch the ground, he was wrestled to the ground and searched.

"Gun!! Gun!!" one trooper screamed out.

All of the other troopers got on high alert. Soon helicopters hovered overhead and the cast iron SWAT truck could be heard in the distance. They were not playing this time. Scar was going back to jail.

Sticks and Trail were detained and released. The cops didn't really have anything on them, and besides, the one they really wanted was Scar, who gave his boys orders to continue running the business until his permanent return, of which he was very confident, this time cleared of all charges against him.

Derek got word of Scar's return and arrest. Watching the media coverage had made his day, giving him a pep in his step. He went back to his cell and retrieved a very important phone number. Then he used his daily phone call to call his new ally.

"Hi, may I speak with Mayor Steele please?" he whispered into the phone, leery of his surroundings. He didn't know who to trust up in the jail and he wasn't taking any chances. He was placed on hold.

When the mayor picked up the line, Derek's heart jerked in his chest with excitement. "Scar Johnson is back," he said. "I want you to watch it all unfold.

When you're ready, I will give you the location of my safety deposit box key with the tape," he whispered. "But first I need your assurance that you will make me a free man once I hand over the evidence you need to bring her to her knees."

"Yes, you have my word. If you have what you say you have, I'm going to need it if I am to take her out once and for all. I love it when a plan comes together. Especially when somebody thinks you're the one in the dark and in fact they are the ones walking blind," Mayor Steele commented.

Derek could feel the mayor's huge smile through the phone. "So we got a deal then?" he asked, himself smiling.

"Yes, we have a deal," Mayor Steele said before disconnecting the call.

"See who gets the last laugh now, you bitch!" Derek mumbled as he walked back to his cell. "I'm back!"

When Rodriguez saw the news report on Scar's return to Baltimore, she was beside herself with anger. She had almost wrecked her car speeding down the streets and highways to the stationhouse like a maniac. When she arrived, she haphazardly parked her car and stormed into the stationhouse. Panting and out of breath, she busted into the cell area and began searching up and down the rows of cells. She didn't see Scar anywhere, which angered her even more.

"Where is Scar Johnson?" Rodriguez huffed, speaking to the little skinny rookie trooper who sat guard at the cells.

"He already went to see the judge for a bail hearing," the little trooper answered.

"A fuckin' bail hearing? There is no way he should get bail! He is a fuckin' flight risk. For God sakes, he just came back into town after being on the run!" she screamed.

As she turned to head down to the courthouse to catch Scar's hearing, she ran headfirst into Chief Hill. The chief had overheard her rant and knew exactly where she was going.

"Rodriguez, I'm warning you. You need to mind your fuckin' business on this one," Chief Hill gritted.

"This is my fuckin' business. My fuckin' sister is dead because of this bastard. You wanna expose me, go right ahead, but believe me, I will not be going down by myself, if you know what the fuck I mean," Rodriguez growled in the chief's face. She pushed past the chief and stormed out of the stationhouse. She wanted to see the whites of Scar Johnson's eyes.

Rodriguez arrived at the courthouse and found out that Scar Johnson's bail had been denied. She sighed. *Maybe Tiphani is done with Scar and she is going to be on the up and up with this case against him,* she thought to herself.

District Attorney Anthony Gill had a permanent hard-on since he'd gotten word of Scar's arrest. Anthony saw this as a golden opportunity to finally bring Scar Johnson to justice for years and years of crime. Anthony had already made it up in his mind that he was not assigning the case to any of the assistant district attorneys that worked for him; instead, he planned on prosecuting the case himself, which was almost unheard of. Anthony knew he'd take some flack from the media, and that his assistant DAs would be mad with him, but he didn't care. His appointment as DA was on the line, and he couldn't risk another foul up with Scar's prosecution.

Anthony sat at his desk studying every single detail and piece of physical and documentary evidence in Scar's case. He wanted every stone turned before he got into court again. His goal was to have so many charges stick that Scar would be in prison for life.

"Mr. Gill, we have just received word from the court on which judge you're going to have for the case against Stephon "Scar" Johnson," his paralegal said in a light voice. She saw Anthony's face and suddenly became nervous.

"Who is it?" Anthony asked, almost holding his breath. He was so nervous, he almost started hyperventilating.

"I'm afraid the judge is going to be Judge Tiphani Fuller," the paralegal said, looking at Anthony.

"Fuck! This shit is ridiculous! Either this bastard Johnson has nine lives, or he is paying out a lot of fucking money to stay on the streets!" Anthony slammed his hands on the desk, knocking over the case file and all the stacks of papers in front of him. Tiphani hated him and had only tolerated his presence at her party because of the mayor.

Anthony's stomach began hurting. This was the worst possible news he could have heard. He was sure Tiphani would let all of the calls in the courtroom go for the defense just to spite him. But one thing was for sure. Anthony would not waste any-more time. He instructed his paralegal to call the courthouse and put in for an immediate start to the trial. He planned on giving new meaning to "the right to a speedy trial."

Scar slipped into his suit jacket. The jury selec-tion for his trial had taken almost two weeks. He had heard through his attorney that Tiphani was being extremely tough on the prosecutor during the jury selection process. He just had to smile to himself af-ter hearing this.

Today Scar was being transported to court to face the revenge-hungry district attorney and, most like-ly, more than half the residents of Baltimore, who all hated him with a passion. He had gotten word that Tiphani was a little pissed at him for getting himself arrested as soon as he returned, instead of coming to see her first. She had wanted him to sneak around and hit her off with some dick before he made his presence back on the streets known. But Scar had other plans. Frankly, he'd grown tired of fucking Tiphani to get what he wanted. Scar was a man who couldn't be held down, and he could tell that Tiph-ani wanted more out of their "thing" than he did. She had even mentioned marriage one time when they had just finished getting busy. Scar thought she was straight crazy for even considering that shit.

Scar wanted to start distancing himself from her, but he couldn't cut her completely off and out of his life until he was a free man.

"Let's go, Johnson," a CO called out.

Scar got his game face on, shrugged his shoulders to shake off his little bit of nerves, and headed out of the cell, confident things would go his way.

Tiphani sat in her chambers preparing to see Scar for the first time since they'd separated from the yacht. She examined herself in the mirror for what must have been the fiftieth time. Kind of nervous about seeing her man after so long, she kept checking her makeup and hair closely to make sure not one hair was out of place. She put on her black judge's robe and struck several different poses. She smiled, made serious faces, then practiced banging her gavel. Tiphani chuckled at herself, behaving like a high school teenager about to go on her first date with a boy she'd had a crush on for years. Finally satisfied that she looked great, Tiphani took one last look in the mirror and winked. She thought she looked very good as a judge. She just hoped that Scar thought she looked as sexy as she thought she did. "Showtime," she whispered to herself.

Rodriguez mixed in with the crowd and settled in on a bench at the back of the courtroom. Her plan was to be present at the trial every single day until she saw Scar get what he deserved. When Sticks and Day walked through the courtroom doors with a few other members of the Dirty Money Crew, she had to count to twenty to keep herself from jumping

over the aisle and beating Sticks until he was uncon-
scious. She knew he was the mastermind of the bank
heist that got Danielle killed and she had something
for him, but first she needed to see Scar get his.

Sticks noticed Rodriguez. He looked over at the
crooked cop and smirked. He hated Rodriguez for
turning Danielle into a snitch. He just didn't know
that Rodriguez hated him just as much. It was definitely a volatile situation in the courtroom that could
explode at any minute.

"All rise. The Honorable Judge Tiphani Fuller presiding," the court officer called out.

"Let the games begin," Rodriguez whispered, eye-
ing Sticks.

Tiphani slid onto her chair. She swallowed hard
and tried to calm down. As hard as she tried, she
couldn't keep from looking over at a very calm and
relaxed Scar, who looked sharp in a charcoal Brooks
Brothers suit.

Tiphani had long since stopped seeing Scar's ugly
scars. In fact, in her eyes he was gorgeous. Just looking at him and thinking about his dick was turning
her on right there in the packed courtroom. She then
looked over at her former boss, District Attorney Anthony Gill, who looked frazzled, like he hadn't slept
in days. She smirked to herself. She could definitely
tell that he was nervous. All the same, she planned
on making his life a living hell in her courtroom.

"Shall we begin? Mr. Gill, you have the floor."
Tiphani looked over at Scar and spoke to him with

her eyes. The message was, *You don't have anything to worry about.*

Scar confidently folded his hands on the table in front of him like he was about to watch a dramatic play or some sort of sideshow attraction. The back and forth between the prosecution and the defense was amusing, to say the least. Even more amusing was the way Tiphani practically abused Anthony on every objection he made, and kept him from asking the state witnesses a lot of pointed questions. Even the reporters in the courtroom had to moan at her overruling of some of Anthony's objections. Tiphani was having a field day.

At the end of the day's proceedings Tiphani raced back to her chambers and locked the door. She ripped off her robe and began touching her clitoris. Her pussy was drenched. She slid her fingers into her own wetness and pleasured herself while she envisioned Scar's muscular body and his thick dick. Tiphani masturbated off the images in her head until she came.

"Oh God. I don't know how I'm going to stand seeing him every day like this. I need him," she mumbled to herself. "I have to make fast work of this trial shit. I need this to be over, so I can get my gotdamn fix," she grumbled under her breath.

Rodriguez had left the courtroom that day sure that she had fulfilled her suspicions about Tiphani's and Scar's relationship. She was very alert to the little glances and smirks Tiphani floated Scar's way.

Rodriguez also noticed that Scar and his attorney were unbelievably calm, even though he was facing enough charges to send him to prison for life. Rodriguez, hell-bent on destroying Scar, was going to continue her hunt to get to the bottom of things, and if Tiphani got in the way, she'd just be a casualty of war.

Chapter 10

Trial and Error

"Your Honor, can we approach the bench?" Anthony Gill was coming apart. His shirt was wrinkled, he looked like he hadn't shaved or cut his hair in weeks, and he had bags under his eyes, hinting he hadn't slept a single hour in the three weeks since the trial had begun.

"Approach," Tiphani said dryly. She couldn't wait to shoot him down on whatever he was going to ask. It had become a daily occurrence in the courtroom to the point where the spectators in the gallery began to look forward to what kind of spectacle she would make out of him every day.

"Your Honor, the State planned on introducing two evidence exhibits today, and, and, well, um—"

"Get to the point, Mr. Gill." Tiphani already knew what he was trying to say, but she had to play dumb.

"Our evidence has gone missing, Your Honor," Anthony blurted out. He looked like he was about to cry.

"Mr. Gill, is this some sort of sick joke?"

"We registered the evidence exhibits with the court as State exhibit 1 and 1a. I'm sure of it; my paralegal has the stamped receipt. But, but . . ."

Anthony was really not doing well. His eyes wide and pleading, he looked as if he would just faint right then and there.

"Mr. Gill, you have made so many errors during this trial, I am very tempted to call a mistrial. Either you get it together, or I'm going to end this circus right here and right now." Tiphani loved the attention of being on center stage and was putting on a show for the courtroom.

In response to Tiphani's berating, Anthony could hardly muster a rebuttal. He just slumped his shoulders in defeat.

Scar's defense attorney pounced on the opportunity to further embarrass Anthony. "Your Honor, with all due respect, we need to continue the trial with or without the State's so-called evidence. It's just too bad the bungling fools at the DA's office can't keep up with their own exhibits."

"I agree. The trial must go on. Mr. Gill, I guess that evidence just won't be admitted. Either find something else, or pick up where you left off." Tiphani had to try very hard to keep a smile from spreading across her face. She felt more powerful than God when she sat up on that bench. Being able to manipulate lives made her pussy wet, and she squirmed in her seat, opening and closing her thighs to create friction around her clit.

Tiphani knew exactly what had happened to the

State's exhibits. She had facilitated the disappearance of two weapons that Scar had allegedly used, one in an assault so severe, a store owner almost died, and the other, he had used to kill a police officer. She wasn't about to let those come into her courtroom.

Anthony Gill rushed back over to his table. His list of witnesses was dwindling. All of the witnesses who were supposed to testify against Scar began backing out when they heard Scar was actually back in town. Anthony was scrambling to keep the case against Scar together and wasn't doing a very good job of it.

Tiphani looked over at Scar and gave him the same little eye signal. Just as she took her eyes off Scar, she spotted Rodriguez staring right into her face. She cleared her throat and held her gaze for a few seconds. Rodriguez's presence at the trial every single day made Tiphani uneasy. She couldn't figure out why she was so interested in Scar's trial. Especially since she had taken dirty money from him.

Tiphani rolled her eyes at Rodriguez and turned her attention back to the trial. She secretly hoped that Rodriguez hadn't noticed her little signals to Scar, but Rodriguez wasn't the only one who noticed.

Day, who was also at the trial most days with Sticks, showing support for Scar, saw the same thing. He and Scar hadn't officially met yet, but they had a history that went way back. As Day sat in the courtroom for another trial against Scar, he couldn't help but get a feeling of déjà vu. The feeling that Scar was going to inevitably get off permeated both trials. He just sat in the trial and thought to himself, *These government mu'fuckas always fuck these trials up. If you want something done right, do it yourself. I'll have to take Scar down myself.*

Rodriguez was convinced there was something going on between Tiphani and Scar. She watched the little exchanges between them and watched Tiphani use the same number of eye blinks each day, the same cough, and a little finger-tap to signal things to Scar. She couldn't prove it yet, but she knew for damn sure that something fishy was going on between Scar and Tiphani, and she planned to continue attending the trial until she got something concrete. She had to be careful before going public with her suspicions, knowing firsthand how far-reaching Scar's power was. She didn't want to end up like the rest of the DES unit—either dead or in jail.

"I am asking that you convict Stephon Johnson on all charges. He is a menace to society. Mr. Johnson has ruined the lives of hundreds of young kids. He has been responsible for ninety percent of the drug distribution on the streets of Baltimore, and he has engaged in bribery, racketeering, and murder. He needs to be off the streets immediately. Only you can do that. The State rests its case," Anthony said to the men and women of the jury in his closing argument. Anthony just wanted the entire debacle to be over. He had failed the city of Baltimore. He was suffering from severe insomnia and had gone home at least four nights, put a .22-caliber in his mouth, and contemplated pulling the trigger. He knew his career wouldn't survive if Scar was acquitted, and he'd been made a fool of enough already.

As Anthony made his way back to the prosecutor's table, he looked over at Scar and shook his head. Without words he acknowledged that Scar was more powerful than himself. He had basically thrown in the towel.

Scar looked over at the jury and saw two members yawn while Anthony was speaking. He chuckled to himself. He felt like the king of Baltimore. Scar was so sure he would get an acquittal, he was unfazed by the proceedings. He even slept with ease in the jail at night because he knew it wouldn't be for long.

Scar's defense attorney barely had to say anything during his closing remarks. He basically harped on the fact that Anthony had bungled the State's case against Scar. It looked like it was working. The jury was attentive, and a few members had even shaken their heads in agreement with the defense. The court proceedings were adjourned while the jury deliberated.

Tiphani raced back to her chambers after she sent the jury out. She paced up and down the floor of her grand office space silently praying that the jury would come back with a quick acquittal. She couldn't wait much longer to have Scar touch her body. As a judge, she couldn't interfere with the jury, but she really wanted to send them a note saying, "Hurry the fuck up."

She jumped when her desk phone rang. "Hello," she answered, anticipation evident in her voice. The jury had reached a verdict. "Okay, I'll be right out," she said. She rushed into her robe so fast, she tripped over it and almost busted her ass. "Calm down, Tiphani, calm down," she said to herself.

Tiphani was back on the bench within minutes of the call. "Jury, have you reached a verdict in the case of the State of Maryland versus Stephon 'Scar' Johnson?" She felt all tingly inside when she said his name.

"Yes, we have." The foreman handed the judge the verdict in a sealed envelope.

Tiphani ripped it open, her hands shaking with anticipation. As she read the words, a hot flash of relief came over her. She handed the paper back to the foreman and immediately gave Scar an eye signal.

"Mr. Johnson, would you and your attorney please rise for the reading of the verdict?" Tiphani stared right into Scar's eyes. She knew right then and there she was definitely in love with him. If she had any doubts before, they had all been erased now.

Scar stood up and adjusted his suit jacket. He looked over at the jury and awaited his fate. Scar's attorney didn't break a sweat. He already knew what it was going to be.

"We the jury find the defendant, Stephon Johnson, not guilty on all charges," the foreman read.

"Noooo!!!" a woman screamed from the back of the courtroom. It was Flip's mother. "He murdered my son! He stole my baby from me." The woman continued to scream, and some of her other family members had to pull her up off the floor.

Rodriguez jumped up and almost impulsively ran up to the front and started beating Scar in his head. Meanwhile, Chief Hill had a huge smile on his face.

Sticks, Trail, and all of the members of their crew who showed up were cheering and exchanging pounds, thinking about the big-ass party that was sure to take place after the trial. Day celebrated with them, but he was thinking of the next step in his mission.

The courtroom was a riotous mess. News reporters raced down the aisles to get the first pictures of Scar. Some snapped quick shots of the defeated and beaten down district attorney. The trial had turned the city of Baltimore on its ass.

"Order! Order!" Tiphani called out. She wanted to officially dismiss Scar, to be the one to tell him he was a free man. The noise in the courtroom quieted to a slight hush as she continued to bang her gavel.

When order was restored, Tiphani said, "Mr. Johnson, the jury has found you not guilty on all charges as listed in the indictment. These charges are dismissed by this court. Mr. Johnson, you are a free man," Tiphani said with another telling bang of her gavel. Scar turned toward the crowd of haters and supporters. He flashed a bright smile, adjusted his suit, and started walking out of the courtroom.

When Scar passed Anthony Gill, he leaned over to him. "Damn, man. Maybe you'll be able to get me in your next life." He let out a loud laugh.

Anthony stared at Scar with a deep hatred. Scar felt untouchable just knowing that his rights under the Constitution against double jeopardy protected him from being prosecuted for the same charges again. He felt like he was as smart as Albert Einstein for the way he had planned and executed his entire acquittal, outsmarting all of these government officials who had big-time degrees from Harvard and Princeton, including Tiphani. He had cleaned up his mess and vowed he'd be more than extra careful from that day forward, which included cutting ties with all of the people around him that he considered deadweight. Like Tiphani.

Tiphani rushed into her chambers, grabbed up her cell phone, and began dialing Scar's phone number. She couldn't even wait until he left the building before trying to contact him. She got the computerized voice mail on Scar's phone. She disconnected the call and redialed again. Again, Tiphani didn't get an answer. She called again and again.

"Okay, Scar, I know you're celebrating, so I will wait for a little while," Tiphani mumbled out loud, tossing her cell phone onto her desk when she really wanted to scream.

"I fuckin' knew it! I knew this bitch was dirty!" Derek screeched as he got news of Scar's acquittal. When he had learned that Tiphani had been appointed circuit court judge and then was miraculously assigned to Scar's case, he became very suspicious of all of the past occurrences. He had sat in his cell for an entire week and written out all of the events involving Scar and Tiphani. Since Derek had nothing but time on his hands, he was able to examine the events one by one, and eventually, like a puzzle, it all came together for him.

Derek placed his last call to Mayor Steele, who did as Derek instructed. The mayor was kind of skeptical when he retrieved the DVD from the safety deposit box, but when he put the DVD into the player, he was pleasantly surprised to see Scar fucking Tiphani's brains out.

"Aghhh! I got you now, you bitch! You just thought you could threaten me. Now let's see who has the upper fucking hand," Mayor Steele spoke out loud to the TV screen as he admired Tiphani's firm titties and round ass. He shuddered, just thinking about how good her pussy felt to him when they'd had their affair. "If your husband only knew what I used to do to you," he whispered, talking to Tiphani's sexy image on the screen. "Well, now he and I are going to destroy you."

Chapter 11

Fatal Attraction

It had been five days since the trial had ended, and Tiphani still couldn't reach Scar. She was having difficulty concentrating on the case before her. In fact, after Scar's acquittal, she wasn't even interested in being a judge anymore, adjourning her cases and giving short breaks so she could go into chambers and call Scar over and over again.

But Scar wasn't accepting her calls. Either that, or he'd gotten a new phone number. She looked at the call history on her phone. All of her outgoing calls were filled with Scar's number. Not even a call to her babysitter or any of her friends was listed.

Tiphani was becoming undone. She wore her hair pulled back into a dirty, ratty bun, and she barely wore makeup these days. She was beginning to feel like Scar was purposely avoiding her, which made her feel like she was going to slip into a deep depression any day now.

She decided she wasn't going out like that. She wanted and needed Scar, and that's what she was going to get. Tiphani went back into the courtroom and adjourned all of her cases being presented for the rest of the week. She had places to go and someone to see, and she wasn't going to stop until she did.

Scar looked down at his buzzing phone for the one hundredth time that morning. "This bitch just won't give up," he mumbled as he rolled over and moved the arm of the beautiful young girl sleeping next to him so he could stand up. He was thinking about changing his cell phone number but had more urgent things to take care of, like running his empire. Scar was sick and tired of Tiphani blowing up his phone like a mad woman. She had left him at least twenty desperate messages begging him to call her back, and not once did she get a return call. Scar didn't feel one ounce of remorse for not calling her, or not wanting to have contact with her.

Scar mumbled to himself, shaking his head in disgust. "Did this bitch really think I would wife her after she cheated on my brother with me? She suppose to be so fuckin' smart, but she couldn't figure out I was using that dumb ass." As he thought more and more about it, he had to smile. He didn't realize his dick could be that powerful. "Maybe I should sell my shit." He chuckled to himself.

Scar was done with Tiphani. Now that she had served her purpose, he didn't need her any longer. Scar was hoping she would've gotten the drift by now, but since she was still calling, he knew she was still on it like that. "Don't tell me I'ma need a fuckin' exterminator for this pest." Scar sighed, looking down at yet another call.

Tiphani sat in her chambers after her day in court. She could barely keep her eyes open. She had been spending her nights sitting outside of some of Scar's old spots and still had not spotted him. It seemed to her like he had changed up all of his regular hangouts and drug houses. It was getting to be too much for her to handle.

The thought of Scar avoiding her was driving her insane. It got to the point that she had been crying so much, her eyes were swollen. Then she lied to her court clerk, saying, she was having an allergic reaction to something.

Again, she called Scar. This time she was crying so hard, her face was a mess of makeup and tears, and she could hardly see the number pad on her phone. "Scar, why won't you call me back? I need to see you right away. Please, please!" she whined into the phone, leaving yet another message on his voice mail.

Tiphani was beginning to feel like a fool. She had given up her entire family, sent her husband to jail for crimes he did not commit, and changed her entire career, all for the attention of her own brother-in-law. She was starting to realize that her priorities had been all fucked up. Now Scar was acting as if he didn't even know her.

She pulled her hair and bit her lip until she drew

blood. "If he thinks he is rid of me that easily, he is fucking wrong. He has not seen the last of Tiphani Fuller," she spoke out loud to herself. Tiphani just had to come up with a plan to get Scar to see her again, and she knew exactly what drove his every thought too. Money.

Rodriguez sat outside the courthouse in an unmarked police car. She watched as Tiphani left the building and got into her car. Rodriguez waited for her to pull out and was on her ass, following her to several different houses and clubs in the seediest parts of town. Finally, Tiphani jumped on the highway. She was heading toward one of the richer parts of Baltimore. Rodriguez was confused, until she saw Tiphani pull up to the gates of a huge mansion.

Rodriguez followed and parked her car down the street. She was going to sit there and wait to see if Tiphani came out with her man. This was her only mission in life, and she had nothing but time. She pulled out her camera and began snapping pictures of Tiphani as she got out of her car and walked up to Scar's door.

When Scar pulled back the door, Rodriguez was able to zoom in and get a great shot of Tiphani throwing her arms around Scar's neck and kissing him deeply.

"That's the money shot, bitch!" Rodriguez said to herself. Within no time she definitely had what she'd come there for.

***

"Oh my God!" Tiphani screamed. "I thought I would never see you again, baby. Why haven't you been answering my calls?" She held onto Scar like she never wanted to let him go, her heart thumping wildly with excitement. If she got caught at Scar's mansion, it would mean the end of her career, and probably her freedom, but Tiphani didn't care. She felt she had been forced by Scar to take this chance. If he had just answered her calls, she wouldn't have gambled like this. Seeing and touching Scar, Tiphani felt like she'd cream in her pants right there on the spot.

"I needed some time to myself. I mean, damn, I just came off trial. Plus, I figured you would be more worried about your kids and spending time with them, since you were away from them for so long."

The only reason Scar had agreed to see Tiphani was because she had left him a message telling him she knew a foolproof plan to make a large sum of money at one time. She had said it would be enough money that Scar could retire from the street life. When Scar heard that, he didn't call her back. Instead, he made Sticks call her and tell her to meet him at the mansion. Scar was about to sell the mansion anyway, so after he used her once again, he would be gone without a trace or a forwarding address.

"I need you. I need you to touch me, baby. It's been so long, and we've been through so much. I did all of this for you. Please . . . Scar, I need you," Tiphani pleaded, rubbing on his dick through his pants.

Scar hated bitches that whined and begged. She

was like a desperate drug fiend. He grabbed her wrists roughly and removed her hands from his body. "You came here to talk about business right now, so let's talk about that." He released his grip on her and shoved her away.

Tiphani crinkled her forehead. She couldn't understand his rejection. She figured the faster she gave him the information she had, the faster he would give her what she wanted. "I had this case come across my desk," she began.

Scar was listening attentively.

"There are several armored trucks coming into the capital building at night, every night. These trucks are filled with all of the government money from each little city in Maryland. I'm talking millions of dollars. The trucks all come together. It's about six of them. I've been told that each truck holds at least ten million dollars. They make deposits into the state's treasury vault. Two of the trucks make deposits to the state's gold repository, so the trucks with a certain insignia also have gold bars inside. The market for gold is unbelievable right now."

"But what makes you think they don't have the entire fucking army coming with those trucks?"

"Because the case involved one of the guards, and he gave up all the details. He said there were only a few guys guarding the trucks. He was suing the government because he got hurt on the job and was saying the government put him in harm's way." Tiphani was desperate to get Scar back in her life.

"How am I going to be able to plan this out? I mean, we need times, dates, amounts, types of guns, all that shit," Scar said, already calculating the money.

"I'm going to help you, baby. I'm going to help us," Tiphani said softly.

"I missed you, girl," Scar lied, grabbing her and pulling her into his chest. He knew just what to say and do to wrap Tiphani around his finger.

A feeling of relief came over Tiphani's entire body. She hugged Scar tightly and began to cry. "Please don't leave me like that again," she cried into his chest. "I love you so much, Scar Johnson."

Scar stroked her hair, but behind her back, he rolled his eyes. He really couldn't stand her weak, silly ass. Sometimes he still couldn't believe he would probably never speak to his brother again all because of this trifling bitch.

Tiphani moved out of Scar's embrace and dropped to her knees in front of him. "Please, let me taste you. I've missed you so much," she whispered. Then she took his thick black manhood into her warm mouth.

Scar inhaled deeply. Her head game was on point. He let Tiphani suck his dick until he came all over her face. Just another way to degrade her, and she was all for it. He looked down at her as she rubbed his cum all over her lips and tongue.

"You want some of this dick up in you now?" Scar huffed.

Tiphani shook her head and rushed to take off her clothes. Scar grabbed her, manhandling her, threw her onto his desk, and rammed his dick into her so hard, she almost choked on her own saliva.

"Agghh!" she screamed out in ecstasy. That was just what she wanted. She was hoping he would reward her sexually, once she gave him the information.

Tiphani was elated to be back in Scar's good graces and never wanted to be without him or his dick ever again. But for Scar, no matter how good she made him feel sexually, he still had it in his mind that he would get the armored truck information from her, and that would be it. Besides, although it was all a part of his plan, now that she was a judge, she was too much of a liability to have around.

Tiphani had barely left Scar's mansion and he was already back to business.

"Yo, Sticks," he called out.

Hearing Scar call his name, Sticks immediately jumped and ran into Scar's office.

"What's that dude's name you grooming?" Scar asked as Sticks entered the room.

"You mean Day?"

"Yeah, that nigga. Tell him I want him to follow Justice Fuller and report back to me with what he sees."

Sticks looked confused. "Who's Justice? I don't think I know that nigga."

"You stupid mu'fucka—Tiphani. Justice Fuller is Tiphani. She a judge, so you call her *justice*. Niggas these days are stupid."

"Oh, word," Sticks replied, embarrassed. "A'ight. I'll holla at him."

"Now get out my face!"

Sticks just turned around and walked out. He thought it best just to shut up and do what he was told before he made himself look like more of a fool.

Scar, intrigued by Tiphani's information, had Day follow her to make sure nothing would get in the way of his chance to live the rest of his life on some tropical island.

Chapter 12

Watch Your Back

Day walked up behind Tiphani in the parking lot of her local supermarket. He had been following her like Scar wanted, but it was also to his benefit as well. Here he could get on Scar's good side and at the same time gather information to destroy him.

"Justice Fuller," Day called out.

Tiphani turned around to see who was calling her. She loved it when people recognized her on the street, and especially when they referred to her as Justice. It actually kind of turned her on. "Yes?" she replied to the stranger.

Day said quietly, "Justice Fuller, I am an associate of Scar Johnson."

Tiphani got nervous. She looked around to make sure no one had heard what was just said.

Day added, "He informed me that you will be gathering information regarding some armored vehicles."

"Who did you say you were?" she asked, not wanting to give any information to a stranger.

"I work for Scar. He and Sticks are grooming me. Scar told me what you are doing, and I want to do it for you."

"Oh, you want to take my glory and get in good with your boss. Well, I promised my man I would deliver, and I will."

"No, I don't want to take credit for it. I just want to make sure you are out of harm's way. See, Scar told me he was concerned for you. He is afraid you will get caught. I just want to ensure that you don't. Yes, I want to keep Scar happy, not by giving him the information, but by keeping you safe. You see he loves you." Day was playing on Tiphani's emotions, knowing how much she loved Scar.

Tiphani was beside herself. There was nothing in the world she wanted to hear more than that. "Did he say that—he loves me?"

"Yes, he did," Day said, laying it on thick now. "That's why I propose that I gather the information, but you can relay it to him. That way Scar stays happy because you are safe."

Tiphani thought it over in her head for a few seconds. She could keep Scar happy by being safe and also giving him information that would make him tons of money. Then he would keep fucking her like she wanted. But what she thought of most was that Scar said he loved her.

"Okay. If it will keep Scar happy, let's do it. I don't want my love to be too worried about me. But I will lock your ass up if you try and take credit."

"I won't, I promise. I'm just trying to make my cash, and it's easier to do that when the boss is happy."

After exchanging a few more details, they agreed on a meeting place and time when Day could gather all of the information from Tiphani. Day walked away happy that he now had more control of his position in the crew, and Tiphani walked away thinking about how in love she and Scar were with each other. In Tiphani's mind they were going to be the ultimate power couple.

Scar was banging into Tiphani's ass from the back. This time she had on her judge's robe. The black material hung around her hips while he moved in and out of her rapidly.

"Who fucks you the best, Your Honor?" Scar said.

Tiphani couldn't even answer him, she felt so good.

Scar felt the nut building up, so he quickly pulled his dick out and squirted his load all over her robe. "Now, that's that reverse Bill Clinton shit! Fuck justice!" Scar said, laughing as Tiphani collapsed on the bed.

Tiphani and Scar had been meeting up in some of the seediest parts of town to ensure that none of her professional colleagues saw them together. It had been a week since he'd accepted her back, and she had been getting fucked lovely every day since. Scar had even fucked her one time in his truck in a dark-ass alley in the hood. Tiphani could care less, as long as she was getting the dick.

"So what's up with that info?" Scar knew her mind

would still be cloudy from the good sex, so she would tell him everything he needed to know.

"I drew you a little diagram," she said, laying on Scar's chest now. "It has the times, which guard has what weapon, their whole routine."

"That's wassup. I knew it was a reason I always thought you was the shit." Scar really did think she was smart, but he didn't respect her one bit.

"So when is it going down?" she asked, leaning up on her elbow and looking into his face.

"We doin' the shit tomorrow night, if everything is gravy. I'm sending my crew out there to scope shit out tonight. As soon as I get the word from them, we will set shit into motion."

"Oh, so you don't trust me and my information?" Tiphani pouted, a little offended.

"C'mon, baby girl. You know me better than that. I'm a thorough nigga. It's business, not personal."

"All I want is ten percent of whatever the take is."

Tiphani had kind of thrown Scar off. He wasn't really expecting to give her shit, but her demand made him have slightly more respect for her.

"A'ight, ma. We can do that. You better get a foreign bank account. Shit, ten percent of millions is gonna be hard as fuck to hide. You damn sure can't stuff those kinda stacks under your bed."

Tiphani hadn't thought that far ahead, but Scar was right. She needed to open her foreign bank accounts immediately. She didn't plan on staying in town after the heist anyway. Her heart was set on disappearing with Scar and her kids to start a new life somewhere with beautiful beaches and constant sun.

***

Rodriguez took more pictures of Tiphani coming out of the seedy short-stay motel. "Damn, Tiphani, you have reached a new low over dick. You and your little boyfriend will be very sorry," she said aloud, as if Tiphani could hear her.

Rodriguez put her camera down and picked up the stack of pictures she had just printed out at Wal-Mart. She shifted through all of the pictures of Tiphani and Scar together. She even had pictures of her naked in the back of Scar's truck.

Hell-bent on revenge for her sister's death, Rodriguez knew what she had was so strong, Tiphani would probably do anything to keep her from releasing the pictures to the media.

She flexed her jaw when she spotted Scar leaving shortly after Tiphani. "Fuckin' coward!" She gritted. She still couldn't believe she'd helped them to bring Derek down, something she considered one of the worst mistakes of her life, but since she was the last DES member standing, she had personally taken on the responsibility of getting revenge on Scar, whatever the cost—be it prison or death.

Anthony Gill put the barrel of his .22-caliber pistol in his mouth and pulled the trigger. Part of his brain busted out of the back of his skull, and his body dropped to the floor like a metal anvil. After being publicly humiliated, Anthony saw his life as being over anyway. Already removed as DA, he knew it was just a matter of time before he was fired all together.

Anthony had sent a note to the mayor explaining that Tiphani and Scar Johnson had made a fool of him, that he didn't want to live any longer. He also sent some of Tiphani's old case files, the ones where she had made side deals.

When Mayor Steele received the letter from Anthony a cold chill had shot down his spine. He read it over and over again. Tiphani was ruining lives one by one, and he wanted her out of the way once and for all.

Mayor Steele, in a close race for the senate seat, with the polls showing him behind by only a few points, needed something to bolster him into the limelight, so he would still have a chance to pull into the lead. With dirt like that on the new circuit court judge, he could portray himself as being tough on government corruption, which would give him a fighting chance at winning the senate seat. But since he was the one who'd appointed her, the situation was a delicate one.

The mayor had been trying to wait before revealing Tiphani's secret, keeping it as a trump card. He really didn't want the evidence to leak out. As he had always done, he wanted to make a behind-doors deal to get her out of the way for good. But as the race went on, he needed a smoking gun, and it looked like Tiphani was holding it.

I'm not waiting anymore, he thought. *Fuck this bitch. Now my friend Anthony is dead because of this bitch. Her husband is in jail. This bitch is like a black widow spider, and I'm about to cut off all eight of her fucking legs.*

"Marsha! Marsha!" the mayor called out.

The young intern rushed into his office. "Yes, sir," she huffed.

"I need you to send out all of these packages with a return receipt. Do not open them and do not fuck this up!"

"I won't, sir. Yes, sir." Marsha took the stack of oversized manila envelopes from the mayor and rushed out of his office. Once she was on the elevator she read the addressee information on each envelope: NBC; ABC; CNN; FOX. She could only wonder what was inside those envelopes.

Mayor Steele needed to get Tiphani's phone number. After being appointed to the judgeship, she had changed her cell number. He wanted to let her know which day to watch the news, so when the world saw her bare naked ass, she would too.

***

When the CO came to the cell to tell Derek he had a visitor he was shocked. He knew damn sure Tiphani wouldn't be coming to visit him again, and he didn't have anyone else. All his friends were either dead or had turned on him.

Derek's mind raced as he followed quietly behind the CO. When he finally walked into the visiting area, his jaw almost hit the floor.

"Let me just start by saying I am so sorry," Rodriguez said in a low, remorse-filled voice.

Derek sat across the table from his visitor, at a loss for words. If there weren't so many COs around, he might've jumped across the table and tried to strangle Rodriguez to death for turning her back on him.

"It's all a part of the game, I guess," he replied.

"I'm here about Tiphani. She is into some heavy shit—"

"I already know all I need to know about that conniving bitch. It was all of you that didn't believe me when I said I was being set up."

"I need your help. I need to know what makes her tick. I need to know everything about her. She was the judge on Johnson's case, and all along she was fucking him."

"That's old news. She was fucking him, and I busted them. That's what started this whole fuckin' war to begin with. Unfortunately, me, Cassell, Archie, and Bolden ended up being casualties. You were our only hope, but you let them convince you to turn on the DES," Derek growled. The more he thought about it, the angrier he got.

"I swear, I didn't know. I didn't know who to trust. I am sorry. I had to take care of my sister," Rodriguez said, her eyes welling with tears.

"What does she have to do with this?" Derek asked softly.

"She has everything to do with it. My mother couldn't afford to take care of her, to keep a roof over their head, none of that. They needed me. She was sixteen, and they killed her, Derek!" Rodriguez whispered, hot tears in her eyes.

"Who killed her? Scar?"

"Scar's little crew. I think he ordered the hit. They may have found out she was my sister. I swear I will not rest until that mu'fucka Scar is dead or in jail for the rest of his black-ass life. And, Tiphani, she is going down with him. She made it easy for him—all over some dick," Rodriguez said through clenched teeth.

"I can tell you everything you want to know about her, but you gotta promise to help me win my appeal."

Rodriguez extended her hand for a shake. "Deal."

They had struck a deal, but they didn't realize that, in the Baltimore County jail, the walls had ears.

Derek was feeling good on his way back to the tier after his meeting with Rodriguez. He had his fellow officer on his side and the mayor. He was sure he would make it out of jail before he could be sent to the state penitentiary.

As he walked along with a smile, he noticed that the CO took a different turn than their usual path to the protective segregation unit. The CO was new, one he hadn't seen in the jail before. "Yo, ain't you goin' the wrong way?" he asked.

The CO didn't answer.

They turned another corner, and suddenly—blackness. Derek tried to scream, but he had a pillow case put over his head.

"They told you to watch your back, nigga!" his attacker mumbled.

The next thing he felt was cold metal piercing the skin of his back, arms, legs, and neck. Derek had been stabbed with a shank over forty times and was bleeding all over his body.

When the deed was done, the fake CO shed his stolen uniform and rushed through the hallways to the escape route his inside contact had given him. He was outside in no time.

He picked up his cell phone and called a very important person. "Yeah, it's done," he said. "Where do I go for my paper?" Satisfied with the answer, he hung up.

Chapter 13

All Good Things Come to an End

Sticks and Trail lay side by side in the bushes on the side of the state capitol building in their assigned positions. Scar had given all of the crew members detailed assignments.

Trail's heart began hammering in his chest when, like clockwork, he saw two armored trucks pull up to the building. And just like Tiphani had said, the armed guards were all laughing and playing around as they unloaded the bags of money. Sticks got up on his knees for a better view.

"Get down, nigga," Trail whispered.

Sticks, anxious to play cowboys and Indians with the guards, ignored him. He was an attention-seeker for real, and he loved a good shootout, but that wasn't part of the plan.

Trail was pissed. He added this incident to a laundry list of shit he wanted to tell Scar about Sticks.

Sticks and Trail watched as two of the armed guards disappeared into the building, while the others hung around talking shit outside.

Trail saw the two black Suburbans approaching in the distance and took that as his signal. Staying low, he quietly ran across the grass and grabbed the guard with the shotgun around the neck, from the back. The guard didn't have time to react, his air supply completely choked off by Trail's tight grip rendering him completely powerless.

Sticks did the same with the other guard, who held a long gun. Except, Sticks used a safari knife to cut his throat.

That wasn't part of the plan either. Trail almost threw up from all of the blood.

Just like a well-run assembly line, their plan fell into place perfectly. As soon as Sticks and Trail had the two biggest threats down, Scar jumped out of one of the Suburbans and shot the other two guards with his Glock, muffled by his homemade silencer.

Then the little young'uns jumped into the back of the armored trucks and began grabbing bags and bags of loot.

After about five minutes, the other two guards were seen talking as they came back out of the building. They immediately noticed that something was wrong. In unison, they both went to draw their weapons, but it was too late. They were ambushed on either side by Timber and another little young boy.

It all happened so fast. All of the guards were dead, and the area looked like a horror film massacre scene, with blood everywhere. Scar had made sure Day got rid of the building's outside surveillance camera prior to the setup.

Everyone piled into the Suburbans, and they raced away from the scene, the SUVs filled with cash.

"Yo, I thought that bitch said it would be six trucks?" Sticks was still on a high from the murder he had committed. But he didn't think they had enough money from just the two trucks. A bunch of people had to get a cut, and he knew Scar would be taking the lion's share.

"Six trucks or two trucks, we got paid, nigga, so stop complaining," Timber said.

Some of the other little crew members started laughing. Nobody was showing Sticks the same respect since Scar's return.

"Who the fuck you talkin' to?" Sticks growled, feeling the heat of embarrassment rising in his chest.

"I'm talkin' to you, bitch-ass nigga!" Timber barked.

Sick and tired of Sticks' shit, some of the others instigated the situation, chanting, "Ohh!"

Timber went on talking to another crew member about the money.

Suddenly, *Bang! Bang!* Two shots rang out inside the truck. Timber's body slumped down in the backseat. Everybody in the truck knew he was dead.

Day almost swerved off the road. "Yo! What the fuck, nigga?" he screamed, his ears ringing.

"You asking questions, or you driving? You can be added to the list of niggas that got caught by the Grim Reaper, if you want to," Sticks said calmly.

When the crew arrived back at the warehouse, Scar

got out of the other Suburban. No one dared to say anything to him.

"Where is everybody?" Scar asked when he didn't see Timber.

There was silence.

Finally, Sticks stepped up. "I had to murk that nigga, boss. He was talkin' about all the shit he was gonna do with his paper and I saw him as more of a liability than an asset. A nigga that run his mouth like that ain't worthy."

The other little young'uns looked around at each other in amazement, but they were too scared to tell Scar the real story.

"My nigga. Always lookin' out," Scar said, giving Sticks a pound. "Now let's count up this paper."

They unloaded the bags and poured out the money on the floor of the warehouse.

"Daaammn!" Scar exclaimed, looking at all of the money stacks. They had to have at least two million dollars in stacks of big bills there. The money had come from so many places and was unmarked.

Tiphani had come through for real. Scar was smiling from ear to ear. He was so happy, he even contemplated keeping her around a little while longer. He picked up his phone and called her.

Tiphani put a hundred-dollar bill between her ass cheeks and told Scar to take it out with his mouth. She giggled like a high school girl when he followed her instructions.

"I always wanted to be able to have enough money

to wipe my ass with it," she said, laughing even harder.

Scar climbed up behind her and swiped his dick up and down her ass crack.

"I'd much rather wipe my ass with that though," she purred.

Scar parted her ass cheeks and wet her asshole with his spit. As Tiphani arched her back and lifted her body to accept him, he slowly eased his dick into her anal opening.

Tiphani bit down into the pillow, and tears leaked from the sides of her eyes. The pain shooting through her ass was almost unbearable.

But the more of his manhood he put in, the better it felt to her. Soon, she was matching Scar pump for pump, and he was moving in and out of her asshole with ease, like it was her pussy.

Tiphani reached under her stomach and put her fingers into her vaginal opening. Having both holes filled made her go wild. She bucked and slammed into Scar even harder now, sending the money that surrounded them on the bed flying all over the place.

"Agghhhhh!" she screamed. Her body shuddered and she fell onto the bed. She'd just had the best orgasm of her life.

Scar was next. "Arrgghh!!" he growled, shooting his load into her tight asshole.

Tiphani lay almost paralyzed on the bed, and Scar fell to the side next to her. She smiled to herself, feeling like her life couldn't be more perfect. She had already made her deposit into her overseas account in the Cayman Islands and was enjoying the fruits of her labor.

***

Sticks waited outside of Trail's baby mother's house. He watched as Trail kissed his little girl and his baby mother at the door. He felt a pang of jealousy. He didn't have any family, and he couldn't hold down a relationship after what happened with Danielle.

Sticks had been watching Trail ever since Scar had told him that Trail was complaining about him behind his back. The crew had another job planned for that night, and Sticks just didn't trust him.

Trail skipped down the front steps of his house, feeling good. He had money stashed now, to take care of his two favorite girls. Trail had come a long way in the game, but after the heist tonight, he planned on getting out and moving far away from Sticks, Scar, and the entire Dirty Money Crew. Preoccupied with his thoughts, he wasn't looking at his surroundings. He went to open his car door.

Sticks stepped from behind it. "What up?" he said, appearing out of nowhere.

Trail jumped so hard, he dropped his keys. "Nigga, what the fuck is you doin' sneaking up on a nigga like that?" Trail could feel his heart beating in his throat. He didn't trust Sticks either.

"What? You ain't happy to see me?" Sticks asked with an evil smile. "Let's take a ride. Scar wants us to do a job," he lied.

"He didn't hit me and tell me shit about a job. What kind of job?" Trail could barely get his nerves under control.

"Just c'mon, nigga. Get in the car. Follow my lead."

Sticks moved his shirt slightly to show Trail his gun, and Trail reluctantly got into his car with Sticks.

Sticks gave Trail directions, a left here, two rights there, and finally they ended up riding down a desolate one-lane road in the country part of Baltimore.

"What the fuck is this, nigga? What could Scar possibly have out here?" Trail asked, looking around.

"We suppose to do a pickup. Scar didn't wanna risk shit getting out in the city," Sticks lied again. "See that car up there? That's them niggas we suppose to meet up with. Pull right behind that car."

Trail felt slightly better. At first, he thought Sticks was doing some snake shit, but when he saw a car parked ahead of them, a feeling of relief washed over him, and he thought maybe Sticks was telling the truth.

Trail stopped his car behind the parked vehicle. "Yo, it don't look like nobody in that shit." He squinted to get a better look.

The next thing Trail felt was cold steel up against his temple. He jumped, and his first instinct was to reach for his own burner.

"Don't even try it, mu'fucka! Get the fuck out the car!"

"Yo, nigga, you on some real bullshit," Trail said, raising his hands.

Sticks kept the gun on Trail, reaching around and taking Trail's gun from his waist. "Now get the fuck out the car!" he barked again.

"Just tell me what the fuck you want, and let's get this shit over with, nigga."

"You a bitch-ass nigga. I heard you was running

your trap about me. You think I'm a power-hungry mu'fucka, huh? Well, you know what . . . you're right." Sticks slammed his gun into Trail's head.

"Agghhh!" Trail screamed out as blood spurted from his head. He fell to the ground, holding his head.

Sticks stood over him. "Stand up and face me like a man."

"Yo, nigga, I don't want no beef with you, man. You can have whatever you want. You want my share of the loot, so be it." Trail wiped blood out of his eyes.

"Nah, nigga, I don't need your money. Although after I fuck your bitch and kiss your baby girl, I might just take that shit." Sticks laughed like a maniac.

Trail tried to drag himself up off the ground to attack Sticks. He couldn't bear to think about Sticks going to his home and putting a hand on his wifey and baby. "You bitch-ass nigga!" he screamed.

Bang! Bang! Bang! Bang!

Trail's efforts to attack Sticks were short-lived. His eyes popped open wider and wider with each shot that pierced his body. He placed his hands over his chest, and his body involuntarily jerked as the life went out of him.

"Who shot ya? Separate the weak from the ob-so-lete!" Sticks sang the Biggie verse as he looked down at Trail's dead body. He spat on his crew member and got into the getaway car he had stashed there.

Sticks drove back into the city to get ready for their job. He had no remorse, and he was ready to murk any other nigga that tried to get in his way. Including Scar.

***

Tiphani rushed out of her car to get to court. She had a few hearings scheduled that she wanted to get over with. Tonight was her and Scar's biggest heist. She couldn't stop thinking about how much money she would get from this job. In fact, she was hoping it was enough to set her up for life.

Just as Tiphani approached the judge's entrance at the back of the courthouse, she was confronted.

"Good morning, Your Honor," Rodriguez said, stepping in her path.

"Rodriguez, what, what are you doing back here? The police entrance is at the front."

"I'm not here on police business. I'm here on judge business." Rodriguez grabbed her by the arm and pulled her out of the view of the court officers standing guard at the back door.

"Get your hands off of me! What is the meaning of this shit?" Tiphani yelled.

"I know all about you and Scar Johnson," Rodriguez began.

Tiphani opened her mouth to speak, but Rodriguez cut her off.

"Don't try to deny it. I'm not asking you, I'm telling you," she said. She pulled a manila envelope from her jacket. "You might want to take a look at these before you say a word." She handed Tiphani the envelope.

Hands shaking, Tiphani slowly opened the envelope. She became hot all over her body at the sight of the pictures inside. "Where did you get these?" she gasped, barely able to speak.

"Don't worry about that. Just know there are more where that came from. Now, can we talk business?"

"What do you want? If it's money, how much? Just tell me," Tiphani whispered. She was drenched in sweat.

"I want you to set Scar up and help me bring him down once and for all. He killed my sister, he is killing kids on these streets, and he set Derek up."

"How?" Tiphani croaked out, tears streaming down her face. She was caught up. She had no choice but to comply with Rodriguez to save her own ass.

"I want you to tell me where the next heist is going down, so we can have teams waiting. Scar will not make it out alive this time."

"W—w—what about me and my children?" Tiphani whined, a mess of tears, sweat, and nerves. "We won't be safe if I give you the information."

"Scar won't know it was you that snitched. I'm not that coldhearted that I'd tell him it was you. But once I help you get away from him, you have to help me free Derek of all the charges against him. Tiphani, you and I both know he is innocent."

Tiphani hung her head. Her so-called good life and fantasy love life was falling apart right before her eyes. With pictures like that, she would be thrown in jail for helping Scar get off on his trial. Not to mention, her face would be plastered all over the media as a crooked judge who slept with defendants. Tiphani had to save herself and think about her children.

"Okay. I will help you bring Scar down," she said, barely able to get the words out.

"Good. Let's talk about a plan. This has to happen sooner rather than later. I will not wait another minute to bring him down to his fucking knees."

***

All of Mayor Steele's packages must have arrived at the television networks at the same time. The telephone lines in his office were ringing off the hook. Marsha, his intern, could barely answer one before the other starting buzzing. The mayor had instructed her to take every single call and confirm that the DVD contained in the package was in fact authentic.

Mayor Steele sat in his office smiling. He had cleared his calendar so that he would be able to watch when all the news programs started airing Tiphani's dirty laundry. It wouldn't be long before she was exposed. He had purchased a brand-new suit for the press conference that was sure to follow Tiphani's little unveiling.

The mayor would have to speak out against Tiphani and her crimes. This scandal would put him in the media's eye, and he would get the pre-election boost he needed. Shit was going according to plan. He had already paid somebody in the jail to get rid of Derek.

It was bad enough that the woman he had appointed to circuit court judge was corrupt. There was no way he could risk Derek revealing that he, the mayor of the city, had struck a deal with a convicted dirty cop, who was a cop killer himself. In Mayor Steele's assessment, Derek should be dead, or at least, that is what he had paid for.

"Yo, man, I saw her talking to a cop, my nigga. I'm telling you, Scar, it was her," Day said.

"Nigga, you better have yo' fuckin' facts straight," Scar barked as he paced the floor.

"I'm tellin' you, boss. I followed her just like you told me to. She went to that court building, but at the back door. I got out the car and watched her talk to that Puerto Rican bitch that was coming here before. She was crying and shit, and then after a minute, she shook hands with her."

Scar punched a hole in the wall. He was angry at himself for letting Tiphani back near him. "I should have trusted my first instinct after the trial and dead-ed that bitch! I had a brand-new start, and I let this dick-hungry bitch weasel her way back in. She is as good as dead."

"Yo, nigga, let me take care of that bitch," Sticks ranted. "I can't tell you how much I wanna murk that bitch. She been a casualty in my book."

"Nah, I got something else in mind for her," Scar growled. "I want everybody to gear up. Tonight is gon' be bigger than I expected."

As Scar continued stalking up and down the warehouse, all of his little workers were silent. No one dared to even make eye contact with him. They knew he was highly unpredictable when angry, and no one wanted to be the one he took his anger out on.

Scar made his way back to his office and sat at his desk, his blood boiling that, against his better judgment, he let Tiphani back into his life. He hated being lied to. He demanded loyalty, and if he wasn't getting it, then that person deserved to die.

"Boss, can I say something else?" Day stood in the doorway to Scar's office.

"Nigga, what? I ain't in the mood, nigga."

"A'ight, when you ready," Day said in his most soothing voice. Scar was volatile, and Day needed him to listen. "I've got a plan to set Tiphani up and pull off the heist at the same time."

"Nigga, I'm always ready. Speak."

Day proposed, "I was thinking I could find Tiphani and tell her the plans of our next heist then make sure she tells that Puerto Rican bitch and flip the script on them bitches."

Scar sat and listened intently, going over the pros and cons of the plan in his head. He liked the idea. He liked it a lot. He gets revenge, and he gets his money. "I like that shit," he said, a sinister grin on his face. "Get Sticks and go find that bitch."

"I think I should do it alone," Day said. "Not sure Sticks is the man for this job."

The grin disappeared from Scar's face. "What you sayin', nigga?"

"I just think Sticks should stay away from this one," Day said, leading Scar on.

It was a fine line between snitching and just giving information. If Scar thought Day was snitching, then Day's whole plan would be shot, and he would be in danger of being shot.

"Why, nigga? Stop being so cryptic. Just tell me. This ain't no twenty questions." Scar was falling right in line with what Day needed.

"I ain't no snitch, but Sticks has been buggin' lately. Timber wasn't talking about how he would spend his money. He clowned Sticks, and Sticks murked him for no reason. And I don't know for sure, but I think he murked Trail. He's been dropping a few hints around the warehouse."

"I hear you. I've had my eye on that nigga. I have my suspicions about him murdering Trail." With his suspicions about Sticks being confirmed, Scar's body was tensing up.

Sensing he had Scar on his side, Day pushed his luck and went for the one thing Scar would definitely react to.

"But the thing that got me wanting to stay away from him is, I think he's got his eye on your throne, boss. I know you ain't gonna let that happen, and I don't want to get caught in no crossfire when you gotta take that nigga down. He's a loose cannon, boss, and I don't want no part of his craziness."

Scar's heart was about to pound out of his chest, he was so furious. Another person in his life was now betraying him. His brother was the one person he could trust, and he fucked that up by fucking his wife and getting him thrown in jail.

"Fuck that nigga!" Scar growled. "You stay away from him. Do your shit with Tiphani alone. What was said in here stays in here. If I hear that you said even one word of what was said in here to anyone, you as good as dead, nigga. Got that?"

"You can trust me, boss," Day said, trying to appease Scar. "This shit stays in this room."

"Get the fuck out my face!"

Not wanting to push his luck any more, Day got the fuck out of the office as fast as possible. He left the warehouse without speaking to any of the other soldiers and made his way to Tiphani and their meeting spot.

Chapter 14

What Goes Around Comes Around

Tiphani and Rodriguez sat across from each other in a hotel room talking about their plan. Tiphani explained all of the nuances to Scar's methods. She drew a small map and told Rodriguez where each of Scar's henchmen would be posted. She laid it all out, with ease.

Rodriguez grew more and more excited by the minute. It would just be a few short hours and she would have Scar Johnson by the balls once and for all.

"You said Scar killed your sister. I didn't know you had a sister," Tiphani said, changing the subject.

"Yeah, a baby sister. Her name was Danielle. She was a good girl, until she got caught up with that boy. He's a part of Scar's crew. No matter how hard I tried to get her out of it, she didn't listen. When I found out she was running with Scar's crew, doing jobs right along with them, I tried to demand that she stop. That backfired and drove her even further in. They set her up to get killed, probably because they found out I was her sister. I don't have anything left to live for if I don't bring Scar down. It was all my fault. All of this was my fucking fault." Rodriguez ended her rant by slamming her fists on the table. She didn't want Tiphani to see the tears welling up in her eyes.

Tiphani was speechless. She had always pictured Rodriguez as a hard ass, but this emotional side was refreshing. She was more encouraged to help Rodriguez now, understanding her sudden quest for revenge. Besides, she had her money tucked away, and there would be other men to fulfill her every need, so she figured it better to save her own ass and help Rodriguez. *Maybe getting rid of Scar is what I need to get over my shortcomings and my sex addiction,* she thought, feeling better about helping take Scar down already.

"Call him. I want to make sure he is still planning to do the job tonight before I send out all of our resources," Rodriguez told her.

Tiphani knew for sure that the heist was still going down, Day having told her all of the details. Nonetheless, she picked up her cell phone and dialed Scar's number.

"Hi, baby," she sang into the receiver. "I'm at the courthouse getting some last-minute work done," she lied. "Is everything still on for tonight?"

"Yeah, everything's on," Scar replied.

"Ohhh! That's so good. I'm so excited. Can't wait to get more of that cold cash in my hands. Maybe after this we can retire to Mexico or even Africa."

Tiphani was laying it on thick with Scar. A little too

thick for Rodriguez's liking. Rodriguez used hand signals and motioned to her to hang up the phone. Taking her cue from Rodriguez, Tiphani cut her call short.

"He said everything will go as planned."

"Oh, yeah? And what did he say about your share of the money?"

"He said it would be waiting for me," Tiphani replied, lowering her eyes.

Tiphani didn't care that Rodriguez and the state troopers planned on busting up Scar's heist. She had enough money from the first two heists to be comfortable if she had to go on the run with her kids. Tiphani had already moved her money and closed her foreign accounts to make sure that her money was safe and that she could not be implicated in any of the crimes if Scar decided to try to take her down with him. She planned to outsmart all of them, including Rodriguez.

What Tiphani didn't know was that Derek had provided Rodriguez with her social security number and all of her computer passwords. Rodriguez knew where she had wired all of her money, knew every transaction she made with a credit card, and even what types of snacks she bought for her children. Rodriguez didn't fully trust her either, so she was always one step ahead.

Bringing Scar down was only part of the plan. Tiphani wouldn't get away completely free. She would also have to pay. Literally.

***

"Where the fuck is Trail?" Scar asked Sticks.

Sticks was caught off guard. He had always had slight suspicions that Scar had a soft spot for Trail, but he could never really confirm it or figure out why. "That little nigga ain't show up today. I haven't seen or heard from him," Sticks lied.

"Call the nigga. He needs to be here. I'm not trying to do no major shit without one of my majors, you feel me?" Scar gave Sticks the once-over.

Scar wasn't stupid either. He knew Sticks was kind of jealous of Trail, so he'd purposely told Sticks about Trail's complaints to see what Sticks would do. He wanted to test him, see if he was a capable and trust-worthy number two. The bitch-ass thing for Sticks to do would be to try to show Trail some malice, but the man-up type of thing to do would be to have a man-to-man sit-down with Trail. That Trail was missing, Scar felt like Sticks had taken the bitch-ass way out.

When Scar was just seventeen he had fallen in love for the first and only time with a woman named Rita. Rita just couldn't be kept. She was a wild child and loved to party and get high. Rita got caught up but not before giving birth to a son—Scar's son.

"I called that nigga, and he ain't answering," Sticks said.

"It's just not like that nigga not to show up for something as important as this. I better not find out that nigga dipped on us with that fuckin' money." Scar gritted, playing it off.

"He probably did. I told you already, when you was gone, this nigga was tryin'-a take over the game like a one-man show. He even went down on the south side and muddied the waters with those cats, Tango and them. I'm telling you, Scar, you thought that dude Trail was quiet. He was a fuckin' quiet menace and a liability." Sticks wanted so badly for Scar to feel for him like he felt for Trail.

"It's all good. The show must go on," Scar said in a low whisper.

Scar needed Sticks for what he had planned for tonight, but there was no fucking way he would let Sticks slide. As soon as he found out what was up with Trail, he planned to get at Sticks in a deadly way. *This nigga better hope not a hair was harmed on my boy's head, or he is a fuckin' dead man,* Scar thought to himself as he eyed Sticks.

Tiphani sat in front of the police van with Rodriguez. She was shaking like a leaf.

"Why are you so nervous? Didn't you do this same shit to help Scar out?" Rodriguez asked her.

"What same shit?"

Tiphani felt her heart sink into her stomach. With all of the precautions she had taken to help Scar, she'd never thought about the human factor—that somebody could be following her and making note of all of her actions.

"Whatever," Tiphani whispered, looking straight ahead out of the window. She watched as all of the unmarked police cars got into position. She noticed the undercover cops strategically placed near the buildings. Tiphani thought about Scar. She was sorry she had to do this to him. She was truly in love with him, but she was more in love with herself.

"What time do you have?" Rodriguez asked her.

"Ten minutes past ten," Tiphani answered.

It would only be a few more hours before that entire street would look like a scene out of a movie. Tiphani's stomach began to cramp. Then her cell phone rang. It was Scar.

"Hello?" she answered, trying hard to keep her voice from quivering.

"What's up, baby girl?" Scar asked, knowing exactly where she was at.

"I'm just here with the kids about to go to sleep and wait for you to come through," she lied. She closed her eyes as she felt her heart breaking.

"That's good. Tonight is gonna be perfect, so have your bags packed and ready to go. I'm bringing you a couple of million tonight. Fuck being a hundred thousand-*aire*. You gonna be a millionaire," Scar said.

"Good! I can't wait," Tiphani replied.

They hung up the phone.

"Boy, he must really be in love with you, or is it the other way around?" Rodriguez said.

Tiphani, frustrated and nervous, ignored her comment. "I just want this to be over with. I don't even know why you need me here. I'm a damn judge!"

"I need you here as collateral. I couldn't trust you to be somewhere that you could let Scar know what's going on. I've seen your sex sessions with him up close and personal. You are in love with his dick, and up until now, dick has made you do some crazy things—Judge." Rodriguez didn't have an ounce of respect for Tiphani's ass and wasn't pulling any punches.

"By the way, did you start thinking about how we're going to get Derek out of jail? I know you must have some strings you can pull down at city hall."

"I will sort things out when this is all over. But let's get one fuckin' thing clear. After I meet all of your demands, I don't want to see your fuckin' face ever again!" Tiphani was tired of Rodriguez putting all of this pressure on her. All she wanted was to meet her demands so she would turn over that pack of pictures.

Tiphani had fallen asleep in the van when she heard Rodriguez's watch alarm going off. She jumped up and wiped sleep out of her eyes.

"It's time," Rodriguez told her. Awake and wired, there was no way she could even think about sleeping on a night where she was so close to bringing Scar Johnson down.

"You better say a prayer. I know Scar very well, and he is not coming without some heavy artillery," Tiphani told her.

Rodriguez instructed Tiphani to climb into the back of the van, not wanting to risk anyone seeing her face through the windshield. She also instructed her to climb into the back and use a long scope to watch for Scar's arrival. Rodriguez had her men in place, and everyone knew the precise time shit was going to jump off.

Tiphani had warned Rodriguez that Scar was very prompt and thorough when it came to these jobs, the main reason he was so successful at it.

The time had finally arrived. Rodriguez watched through a scope as the armored trucks arrived. Her heart thumped wildly as she watched the drivers and guards unload the bags of money. "Scar and his little band of misfits should be rolling in another minute or so," she whispered.

According to the way Tiphani had explained it, Scar and his little men would hit, once two of the guards had gone in to do the drops. Rodriguez held her breath for a minute in anticipation of Scar's arrival. But nothing happened. She looked down at her watch. It had been almost five minutes since the guards disappeared into the building, and there was still no sign of Scar.

"Where the fuck is he?" Rodriguez asked, growing antsy.

Another two minutes passed, and still no Scar Johnson.

"Officer Rodriguez, where the fuck is your band of thieves?" one of the SWAT guys asked through on the radio. They had been in position for so long, they were tired of waiting.

"He was supposed to be here already," she responded.

More time passed and still no Scar. Now the guards that had gone into the building returned, and all of the guards began preparing to roll out.

"What the fuck did you do?" Rodriguez screamed. "You fucking told him, didn't you? You slimy bitch!" She dropped her scope and grabbed Tiphani around her throat.

"No! I didn't. I—I d—did not," Tiphani croaked out.

Rodriguez continued squeezing her neck. She had lost all control. The opportunity to bring Scar down was slipping away, and she thought Tiphani was responsible once again.

"I will kill you," Rodriguez growled, spit dripping out of her mouth. She looked like she was possessed by a demon. She continued to squeeze until she noticed Tiphani's eyes rolling up in her head. Tiphani made gurgling noises like she was about to die. Rodriguez snapped out of it and let her go.

"*Ahem! Ahem! Ahem!*" Tiphani was coughing like crazy, trying to catch her breath, tears streaming down her face. She instinctively sucked in gulps of oxygen as she held her throat. Everything had gone wrong, but she hadn't tipped Scar off. She was worried that Scar not showing up might mean he was on to her. If that was the case, she knew she'd be marked for death.

Once the armored trucks pulled out, Rodriguez, feeling defeated, slumped down in the back of the van.

"Officer Rodriguez, was this some fuckin' kind of joke?" one of the undercover officers blared through the radio.

Rodriguez ignored the questions that came through the radio one after the other. She felt like a total fool and a failure. Again. She looked out of the van's windshield and noticed that all of the state troopers she had enlisted for the bust began coming out of their hiding spots. Rodriguez guessed it was to discuss what had gone so damn wrong. She knew she had to eventually get out and try to calm them all down, but she was so damn embarrassed, she hesitated.

"You fucked up, Tiphani," Rodriguez said in a harsh whisper. "You are going to be ruined."

"I swear I didn't tell him anything. I wouldn't be sitting her like a sitting duck if I had tipped him off. You have to believe me. I held up my end of the bargain, but something must've happened to keep him from coming here."

"No! Something doesn't just happen! Somehow he must've fuckin' found out!" Rodriguez screamed. "My first guess is, you fuckin' told him, so he would fuck your brains out. My second guess is, you're so stupid, you didn't notice that he fuckin' had a tail on you the whole time."

Just then there was a knock on the van door. They both jumped.

"Officer Rodriguez, it's me!" the SWAT team leader screamed.

Rodriguez pulled back the door and climbed out of the van. Tiphani sat inside listening to their conversation. Rodriguez was pleading for forgiveness, telling the other enraged troopers, she had everything planned out to the minute and didn't know what happened.

One of the SWAT members stepped in front of his boss to give Rodriguez a piece of his mind. Suddenly, the SWAT team leader dropped to the ground, a perfect hole in the center of his forehead.

"Oh, shit!" Rodriguez screamed.

Next, the other SWAT team member fell to the ground. Same thing, a perfect hole. Then two more officers were down.

Rodriguez looked around on the roofs of the surrounding buildings, but she didn't see anyone. Then she noticed a red dot on her arm. She raced to get back into the van. She knew then that there was a sniper firing from somewhere. "Everybody get the fuck back to their cars now!" she screamed into her radio, and all of the officers began scattering.

Scar was once again one step ahead of them.

A bullet whistled through the air and hit the side of the van as Rodriguez was about to climb into the front to drive away. She dropped down on top of Tiphani, who was crying hysterically, to shield her. Then more bullets hit the van, one shattering the passenger side window this time.

"Oh, God! He is going to kill us! What about my kids?" Tiphani screamed, covering her ears.

Rodriguez knew she had to take a chance to get out of there. She jumped into the driver's seat and started the van. Just as she went to pull out, *Bang!* A bullet pierced the windshield, and Rodriguez's body slumped over, blood leaking from her head.

"Agghhhh!" Tiphani screeched. If she didn't act fast, she would never make it out of there alive. From the back of the van, she struggled to pull Rodriguez's limp body from the seat. By now she could hear more police coming onto the scene and more bullets flying. She struggled with the dead weight until Rodriquez's body finally fell far enough over that she herself could climb into the driver's seat.

Tiphani struggled behind the wheel and hurriedly threw the van into drive. With her hands shaking fiercely, she pulled out like a mad woman. Just as she made it out of the spot, another bullet hit the side of the van. They had missed her again. She sped down the street and away from the scene, crying and shaking so hard, she could barely maintain control of the car.

"Oh, God! What have I done? What have I done? Somebody help me!" she squealed. She didn't know where she was going or how she would ever get her kids so she could disappear.

Tiphani kept driving and driving. When she thought she was far enough away from the scene, she picked up her cell phone. That's when she noticed a flashing text message—YOU JUST FUCKED UP. MAKE SURE YOUR WILL IS UP-TO-DATE, BITCH.

Tiphani threw her phone down. She knew exactly who the text was from. Scar was out for revenge, not just any kind of revenge. He would have a high bounty on her head. She couldn't stay in Baltimore. She just had to figure out a way to get out before Scar and his little crew members found her.

Tiphani thought she knew somebody who could help her. She picked her phone back up and dialed the mayor's phone number. The mayor had told her to meet him at the courthouse, that he would gladly help her.

Tiphani watched as the sun came up on another day. She knew it would be her last day in Baltimore, Maryland.

Derek clung to life in the jail's infirmary. The nurse came in and shifted him in the bed, so he wouldn't get bed sores. He'd heard the doctors say he had barely made it.

The small television that hung over his bed had the news on. Derek stretched his eyes when he heard a reporter say that there was breaking news regarding

Judge Tiphani Fuller. He knew right then that Tiphani's indiscretions with Scar would be aired that day beginning on the 6 o'clock news.

Wincing in pain, he fought against the drowsy effects of the painkiller to watch the news. He planned to be glued to the television for every single news broadcast. Derek hadn't figured out who'd tried to kill him yet, but he also planned to await Rodriguez's return with the information needed to help him get free. If Rodriguez didn't come through, he knew he still had the mayor's loyalty for helping him. Derek was happy to still be alive and took comfort in the fact that all of Tiphani's lies would finally be brought to light. In his assessment, he would be a free man in no time, and the first place he would go is to see his brother, eye to eye, man to man.

Tiphani had managed to sneak into a drug store and purchase a Halloween costume wig, some oversized shades, and a new shirt. She couldn't go to the courthouse in a shirt with Rodriguez's blood splattered all over the front of it. She took a cab to the court building, and as she exited, she looked around. Tiphani noticed all of the cameras and the podium set up at the front entrance.

"This is all I need today," Tiphani mumbled to herself. "A fucking high-profile case in front of the court. I need to get inside to meet with the mayor. Just gotta make it inside." Tiphani didn't notice that she was once again being watched like a hawk.

When she got to the back entrance, the guards didn't

recognize her. One court officer told her, "Ma'am, this entrance is for judges only."

"I am Judge Tiphani Fuller," she said nervously, pulling the sunglasses down slightly to reveal her face a little more.

The guard's eyes grew wide, and he swallowed hard. He looked like he'd just seen a walking dead person.

"Stay right here, Judge Fuller, um, one minute."

The guard ran behind the desk and picked up the telephone. He mumbled something into the receiver as he eyed Tiphani, who rolled her eyes at him, tapping her foot impatiently. Tiphani was fuming. She didn't have time for this shit today. It was all too risky standing there. The longer she waited, the less time she had to make it out of Baltimore alive.

"Judge Fuller, they have instructed me to escort you to the front entrance of the building," the court officer told her.

"What? What the fuck is going on?" Tiphani screamed as four other court officers emerged and put hands on her. She began fighting them, bucking and thrashing. "I'm the fuckin' circuit court judge! What the fuck is the meaning of this?" By now her wig had come off, making her identity readily apparent. "You are making a mistake!"

When the guards emerged through the front doors with Tiphani, she was met by a crowd of media and Baltimore citizens. Mayor Steele was standing behind a media podium, all dressed up and looking debonair.

The crowd began jeering and booing Tiphani.

"Murderer!" a lady screamed out.

"Dirty judge!" screamed another.

Tiphani felt her stomach muscles clench. There was basically a mob of people after her. "Mathias, what is going on here?" she shrieked.

"Here she is, ladies and gentlemen. The crooked judge who sleeps around with defendants and gets paid to hand down acquittals," Mayor Steele announced in a serious tone.

"Mathias, I can ruin you!" she screamed.

It was too late. She listened to a loudspeaker blaring her voice. "Aghhh, Scar, fuck me! You fuck me so much better than Derek."

Tiphani's bladder released right there on the spot. The entire world knew she had fucked Scar Johnson and that she had been on the take the entire time.

"Just like I promised, I will be tough on government corruption. There will be no dirty cops or judges when I'm elected to the state senate next week," Mayor Steele boomed into the loud speakers. "Take her to jail where she belongs!" Mayor Steele shouted. With that command, the court officers roughly carted Tiphani to the cells inside the courthouse.

Tiphani was screaming, but no one could hear her over the loud jeers of the crowd, which was now turning into a mob.

Scar watched from a distance. He was pissed. Now he would have to use other connections to get to Tiphani. One thing was for sure, he wouldn't let her get away with setting him up. He had two of her most precious commodities to hold over her head.

"Uncle Stephon, when will we meet up with Mommy?" Tiphani's son asked.

Scar looked at Tiphani's daughter, who was sleeping in the backseat of his truck, Sticks sitting next to her, his gun on the ready. "Soon, baby boy, very soon." He picked up his cell phone to call in a favor.

Chief Hill raced out of the stationhouse. He had received a call that spurred him into action. He arrived at the courthouse in record time, flashed his identification, and rushed to the cell area where Tiphani was being held. "I'm here to pick up our prisoner," he announced. "Judge Fuller."

The captain of the court officers asked, "Who said she is the state's prisoner?"

"I fuckin' said it, and the mayor fuckin' said it. You want to question us? Or maybe Judge Fuller is fuckin' you and payin' you too," Chief Hill gritted through clenched teeth.

The decorated court officer backed right down.

Tiphani was sitting in the corner of the cell when they came in and told her she would be going with the chief. She remembered Chief Hill's face from somewhere, and it wasn't in court. She slowly walked out of the cell and out of the courthouse with Chief Hill, who led her to an unmarked car.

Tiphani thought that was very strange. "If I'm so bad, why don't you have a squad car? And since when does a chief come out to pick up prisoners?"

Chief Hill was silent. He held onto Tiphani's arm tightly as he led her into the back of the car. Once she was seated inside and he was in the driver's seat, he turned on his car radio.

"Uncle Stephon, when are we going to see Mommy?"

Tiphani heard her son's voice coming through the speakers. "Noooo! Help me!" She began to scream and buck in the backseat. She tried banging her head on the windows to get the attention of anyone on the outside, but it was of no use. She continued to scream. "Please! Not my children, pa-leeeessee!"

"No need to cry now, Judge. You brought this all on yourself," Chief Hill said calmly.

Just then it came to Tiphani remembered where she knew the chief from. She had seen him meet with Scar several times to pick up payments. She had also remembered seeing him in the courtroom when Derek was convicted. All along she'd thought of him just as the chief of Division 1, but as it turned out, he was another of Scar's paid aces.

Tiphani knew her life was over. She figured she would never make it to any prison. The chief was surely going to be driving her straight into Scar's hands.

Her throat sore from screaming, Tiphani finally gave up on her cries for help, and began concentrating on trying to ease her hands out of the handcuffs. She kept struggling. She felt like her wrists were bleeding already, which was exactly what she wanted—something wet and moist to help her squeeze her small, bony wrists out of the cuffs. She kept on maneuvering as the chief continued driving.

All Tiphani could think about was her children, who were old enough to identify Scar, so she knew he would kill them too. Tiphani felt a flash of anger in her chest, as her motherly instincts suddenly started taking over, her need to save her children becoming overpowering.

Tiphani had always thought of herself as a shrewd career woman with the skills to keep rising to the top. But now, riding in the back of a cop car with a crooked-ass police chief on her way to meet death face to face, it looked like the "Maryland blues" was bringing her right back down. But Tiphani had other plans. If she was going to die, she would die trying to free her kids first.

As she looked at the back of Chief Hill's head, Tiphani felt like it was now or never. She pulled the handle on the door, and it flew open.

"Oh, shit!"

Chief Hill screeched as he swerved the car, causing him to slow down a bit, all part of Tiphani's plan.

Tiphani jumped out, and her body hit the road like a sack of potatoes and rolled. She could feel her skin ripping open with "road rash," as the wind was knocked out of her. After a few seconds of excruciating pain, she got her bearings enough to run down the highway screaming for help.

Chief Hill pulled over on the shoulder of the highway and got out of his car. He kicked the tires. "Fuck!" he screamed. He scrambled to his car and picked up his police radio. "Chief Hill, Division 1, on the air!" he screamed.

"Go, Chief," the operator answered immediately.

"I have an escaped prisoner on I-95. Female, black— aww, fuck it! It's Judge Tiphani Fuller, and she is to be considered armed and extremely dangerous. I want her taken down by any means necessary! I repeat, she is to be taken down!" Chief Hill barked. If Tiphani got away, Scar would simply kill him, chief of police or not.

Tiphani ran down the highway like a mad woman. Her legs and chest burned as she ran as fast as her legs would take her. "Help me!!" she screeched.

Finally, a long-haul truck driver stopped. He thought maybe the crazy woman was running from a john that was trying to beat her up or kill her. He reached over and pushed open his passenger side door.

Tiphani climbed up into the cab of the eighteen-wheeler. "Please, help me!" she huffed. "I'm a judge. The police are trying to kill me!" she gasped.

The truck driver was stunned, not understanding what he got himself into. Then he noticed all of the police cars whizzing down the highway. "Oh shit! You need to hide up in the back of the cab," the truck driver said with a thick country accent. "I got some blankets back there you can cover up with."

Tiphani did as he said.

"I'm gonna keep on driving the hell outta Maryland, but I know they gonna eventually block off this here road."

"Just keep driving, please. My life is on the line," she cried, burying herself in the back of his cab.

Day was getting nervous. He had been waiting at the meeting spot for half an hour, and still there was no sign of his girl, which wasn't like her. She was always right on time. The war on Scar Johnson was getting heavy, and Day was afraid that his girl had been found out. He vowed to look out for her and keep her safe, and if she wasn't, his guilt might push him over the edge.

Then, out of the shadows she crept. She was being very careful not to be spotted by anyone, and to make sure it was Day in the car.

Day pushed the button to roll the automatic window down. "Get in quick, Halleigh."

Halleigh ran to the passenger side door and got in the car. "Dayvid, I'm sorry I'm late."

Dayvid and Halleigh had met when Halleigh moved to Baltimore from Flint, Michigan. Dayvid was being groomed by Halleigh's man, Malek, to take over his drug business, and the three formed an immediate bond. When Malek had asked Dayvid to take care of Halleigh when he was gone, he didn't need to ask twice. Dayvid would do anything for Malek.

Malek was killed in front of his house with Halleigh watching as Detective Derek Fuller shot him. From that moment Halleigh had vowed revenge on Detective Fuller. After she started following him, she realized Detective Fuller was an associate of Scar Johnson. That's when Dayvid realized that Scar probably had Detective Fuller kill Malek because he was moving in on Scar's territory.

Ever since then, Halleigh and Dayvid had been shadowing Detective Fuller, Scar, and anyone associated with the Dirty Money Crew. They fancied themselves a cross between Bonnie and Clyde, and Robin Hood. They had made a pact and were determined to destroy the persons responsible for the death of Malek, the one person they both loved.

"I followed Tiphani to the courthouse, and shit was

a circus over there," Halleigh told Dayvid. "There were camera crews and reporters everywhere. They grabbed her up and propped her up in front of everyone as the mayor made a speech about cleaning up corrupt police and judges."

"What? Slow down. What happened?"

"They played the tape we made of Tiphani and Scar fucking, right there in front of the whole city on a big screen so everyone could see. Detective Fuller must have leaked the tape we sent him. Holy shit! I can't believe this, Day. Our plan is working!" Halleigh was about to jump through the roof, she was so excited.

She reached over, grabbed Day, and kissed him passionately. Then they both separated and just stared at each other for a second, both stunned by the sudden passion. Before, it had just been more of a business relationship. Although Day definitely had a thing for her, he would never disrespect Malek like that. Not knowing how to handle the situation, he just moved on like it was nothing.

"We need to keep on track. I told you this would work. I have to get back to Scar. You go home, and we will meet up later to figure out our next move. Stay hidden in the shadows. Don't let no one see you."

"Okay." Halleigh got out of the car and ran into the shadows.

Dayvid sat there and watched her disappear. He whispered, "I love you. Be safe."

Derek was elated when he'd heard of Tiphani's arrest at the courthouse. He was just waiting for the day the COs walked into the infirmary to tell him he was a free man. Today, when the COs knocked on the little metal hospital bed to tell him he had a visitor, he just knew it was someone sent by the mayor's office to let him know he would be free in no time.

When the visitor stepped into the room, Derek's heart started racing. It was Sticks who was ambling toward his bed. Derek almost shit his pants. He shot Sticks an evil look. He wasn't fully recovered from the stabbing, so he knew he had no chance of winning a fight with Sticks.

"What the fuck are you doing here?" Derek growled in a low voice, so the guards wouldn't overhear his conversation.

"Scar sent me, nigga. You know the drill. He wanted to me to send you a message. The same strings you pulled to ruin your ex-wife and bargain for your freedom is the same ones you need to pull to help him get out of Baltimore unscathed," Sticks whispered harshly.

"Tell Scar I said fuck him!" Derek spat. He winced. Raising his voice caused him pain.

"I don't think you will have the same attitude once you see this." Sticks dropped some pictures onto Derek's chest.

Derek reached out with his one free hand and picked the pictures up. They were face down. He examined them, almost choking on his own spit as he stared down at pictures of his kids sitting on Scar's lap. He crumpled the pictures as he balled up his fist.

"What the fuck does he want?" Derek gritted, his body throbbing with pain.

"He wants your ex-wife dead. He also wants it to be arranged that he gets out of Baltimore without the beast breathing down on him. Scar knows about your little agreement with the mayor, soon-to-be senator, so he figures you can throw some words his way. It's either that, or receive your kids' body parts one by one as a care package here at the jail," Sticks said with finality. He didn't even give Derek a chance to answer. He just stood up and walked toward the door, and the CO standing guard let him out.

"CO! CO!" Derek called out frantically.

The CO rushed to his bedside.

"I need a phone," Derek said, struggling with his words. "I have an emergency at home."

Tiphani and the truck driver made it through the police road block without a hitch. A few state troopers had climbed up into the truck's front cab to take a look, but they hadn't seen anything. Besides, the smell of the truck driver's cigars and his musty underarms had driven them right back out.

She came out of hiding when the truck driver announced they had made it all the way down to Fort Lauderdale, Florida. She climbed into the passenger seat of the truck and stared out at the water. She began to cry. The reality of her situation had started setting in. She would be spending the rest of her life on the run. Not only was Scar Johnson looking for her with plans to kill her, but every single police entity in the state of Maryland had a bounty on her head as well. As she said a silent prayer for her children, she realized the truck driver had been speaking to her.

"So what you gonna do from here?" he said. "I'm headed back home to Texas to my family."

"I don't know. But if you leave me your name and some contact information, I will make sure you are compensated for all of your help."

"That won't be necessary. Let's just say a guardian angel sent me to save you from the boys in blue," the man said.

Tiphani let a weak smile spread across her face. Then she opened the truck door and climbed out onto the street. She looked around at her new surroundings. She smelled the salt air, looked at the palm trees, and said to herself, "I will have the last laugh, you mu'fuckas," as she walked to the beach to begin plotting her comeback.